I0822910

A SECOND CHANCE

STEVEN TURNER

TABLE OF CONTENTS

CHAPTER ONE

After running seventy-five meters, Anthony only had twenty-five more to go. He zigged and zagged like a running back making cuts on an open football field. This type of running helped him avoid fallen trees, large rocks and the bullets from the gun fire coming from in front of him.. He also had to either jump over or run around the large holes created by the falling mortar shells from the top of the approaching hill along with the large boulders. He was also taught that a moving target that was changing directions was harder to hit.

ZIP ... ZIP ... ZIP .. he could hear the bullets passing by him. Anthony saw that some would hit the sandy dirt with puffs, in front of him or to his left and right as he continued his zigging and zagging. Although the noise of gun fire, mortar shells exploding and heavy artillery guns blasting away from in front of him or coming from behind him, he concentrated on only two important things. His breathing! He could hear himself breathing through his mouth. WHOO ... WHOO ...WHOO. He chugged at full speed through the large field that was just in front of the fairly large hill. It helped him concentrate and plan his next movements.

There wasn't a cloud in the clear late afternoon blue sky. There wasn't any wind either. The air was humid, which made the breathing of the hot air very difficult. Anthony had spent much of his time at Port Royal South Carolina's Marine Boot Camp on Paris Island training for situations just like this. As his soaked clothing from sweat stuck to his body, he continued on.

WHOO ...WHOO... WHOO.. ZIP ... ZIP ... BANG ... BANG... BOOM

His helmet, which was held in place by a leather strap under his chin, bounced up and down. Anthony ran with his M1198 .30 cal Browning Automatic Rifle in both hands. He swung it in a rhythm that matched his breathing.

ESSA ... ESSA ... ESSA.... was the second thing that he concentrated on. He would say it out loud in between his breaths as he ran forward.

Being a little faster than the rest of his Marine Raider squad of ten, he was out in front of the scramble. First Sargent Anthony Rucker would also be the first of the ten to reach the base of the hill that was part of their objective of the mission. Laying low in the sand and dirt mixture on the South Pacific Island of Okinawa, Anthony took his shovel out of his ruck and began digging in.

Thunk! Someone fell on him.

"What the?"

Anthony pushed the body that was partially on top of him. As it rolled off, he locked eyes with Rich Scrivner. Rich's eyes were wide open with a blank stair on them. Anthony also noticed a hole in the side of Rich's head that was draining blood on to the sandy and now red dirt. Rich was gone.

Anthony took some time to stick Rich's Browning Automatic Rifle in the ground and place his helmet on top of it. This was to mark the dead body for those who would come later for those killed in action. First Sergeant Rucker had to gather himself and continue on, doing what he was trained to do. And that was to fight the enemy.

Anthony Rucker had spent six weeks of training at Paris Island with over 5,000 other Marine recruits after the day that Americans would never forget. December 7th, 1941. Anthony knew that after what happened in Pearl Harbor, he must join the war effort, as did the other 5,000 young men.

CHAPTER TWO

Anthony Rucker had grown up in what was called Butchertown in San Francisco California. This part of San Francisco was known for it's tough people. It was an accumulation of many ethnic races. Irish, English, Scots, Italians, French and Mexicans all lived and worked together. The area was twenty six streets that were aligned in alphabetical order from North to South. From what was once called Railroad Ave, it also extended to the East all the way to the edge of the Bay.

Four large slaughter houses lined Evens and Fairfax Avenues. Large holding pens that took up full city blocks held the sheep, hogs and beef cattle that were to be slaughtered. They were also scattered on Galvez, Hudson and Innes Avenues. Tallow works and hide shops were also in the area closer to the edge of the Bay. Up on what was called Bayview

Hill, were large pastures used for for grazing .All of these businesses supported those who lived in Butchertown.

Most San Franciscan's stayed away from this part of "The City". By 1935, the streets of Butchertown finally were completed along with a sewer system, phone lines and electricity to every home. For the previous sixty years Butchertown was a messy, muddy and smelly place that was covered with horse, cattle, sheep and hog droppings. Now, it was just smelly. The animals were no longer aloud on the streets except for an occasional horse and sometimes strays that got out of the holding pens. The combination of several thousand animals and their waste along with the hide factories and tallow works, gave the area a definite personality.

The people who lived there were, what some folks would call "salt of the earth'. They worked hard and played hard. Most of the young men stayed in the area after high school and worked at the different businesses. Pay was good enough to support a family. New housing developments were being built on the old pastures that over looked the Bay. They were affordable and close to work.

Butchertown had its famous people that everyone from there knew. Lefty O'Doul, the most famous of all, was a Big League baseball player that was born on Galvez Ave. He owned his own restaurant in downtown San Francisco called O'Doul's and he was the manager of the Seals, San Francisco's minor league baseball team. He also played big league baseball for the New York Giants . "Big Dick" Abrams was the local police officer along with "Shorty the Cop". Both were ex military guys from World War 1. They now rode around in

Police cars instead of the horses they once rode around on in the twenties and early thirties. Jack Allen was the owner of the largest slaughter house. Cyril DeNike owned DeNikes Tavern on the corner of Third and Galvez. He sponsored many youth athletic teams in Butchertown. Nellie Bloom was a well known horse rider and female rodeo star. Bob Turner was known for his prowess in the hay rings as a bare knuckle fighter.

Anthony Rucker had attended and graduated from Commerce High School in 1940.He was a good student, not a great one, only because nothing really interested him academically. He did love to play football. Being a smaller guy as a freshman and sophomore, he wasn't a dominant player. As a Junior, he became a Varsity starter in the third game on defense and in the fourth game he also started on offense. He was the only player on the team who would play every snap of the remaining games. Although he was the smallest player on the offensive line, he had success by staying low and using really good technique. He often frustrated his opponents because he never gave up and kept coming at them play after play with one hundred percent effort. He practiced with that same effort everyday. He was afraid if he didn't practice hard every day, there was the possibility of losing his position that he worked so hard to get. He understood his advantages and disadvantages. He was quick and in great shape. When the play started, Tony was the first to move making sure he was doing the hitting and not getting hit. By playing low, he avoided the bigger, stronger upper bodies of his opponent. Tony also learned to play with pain, often blocking it out. The next day after games was usually difficult on him. But as his father taught him "You got to do what you got to do, so that you can do what you want to do." And Tony wanted to be on that field all of the time.

Tony, as he likes to be called, was well liked by all of his classmates. He didn't date any girls because he was so shy, but he did have his eyes on one specific young lady. Janessa Kapas! She was the most attractive girl in the school and was dating a Senior on the football team. Tony and Janessa were friends and talked often. They even had one class together. Janessa had glamorous long straight brown hair parted slightly to the right side that came to her shoulders. She had stunning dark brown eyes with long lashes and nicely trimmed eyebrows. Her dainty nose had straight lines that fit her face perfectly. Her blended skin had a brown tint to it that she got from her Italian and Greek parents. Janessa's lips were full with a sultry look. They surrounded an elegant mouth with bright white straight teeth. When she smiled, tiny dimples showed at the corners of her mouth. She had three different smiles. Her most common smile was a very pleasant smile that she almost always had. She had a very, very Happy smile and a sultry smile with a slight head tilt. Those smiles set her aside from everyone. They just made her so pretty. She never wore much make up, because she didn't need too. Janessa's athletic figure included a long neck and also very long shapely looking legs. Janessa walked like the graceful athlete that she was. At that time, girls only competed in their Physical Education classes. She loved to watch all sports, especially football. Along with her beautiful face that included a unique and wonderful smile, she had a witty personality! And her voice was also different. She talked with a little whisper that combined with a little unusual accent. Anthony and Janessa would go back and forth about the silliest topics,always trying to one up each other. For some reason Tony wasn't shy or intimidated by Janessa . She was different than all of the other girls. They didn't even notice him. He found that Janessa gave him a sense of confidence. If she would take the time to playfully talk with him and enjoy it, he shouldn't any longer be afraid or shy around any other girl. To Tony, Janessa was a special person.

To Janessa, Anthony was different from all of the other boys she knew. His simple way of dressing, hid his athletic body. His dark brown eyes with the long black lashes seemed to look right into her. They captured her own eyes and gave her a soothing feeling. She felt relaxed around him. Those eyes were part of what she thought was a very handsome face. Anthony had a self confidence about him that made her also feel safe. His quit strength and fun personality excited her. Janessa could also tell that Anthony was a caring and loyal person. Guys like him were difficult to find.

For some reason, things changed at the beginning of his Senior year. Girls began to go out of their way to talk with him and be around him. He was now six feet two inches tall. His jet black hair neatly cut and combed, combined with an equally black uni-brow, dark brown eyes and eye lashes longer than most girls, gave his face a handsome look. He also had a confident air about him but not a cocky one. The more the girls were around him the more they saw what Janessa already knew. He was also one of the best football players, Team Captain and didn't have a girl friend. Tony was easy going and friendly to all of the students. He had time for everyone who wanted to talk with him. He knew how it felt to be looked down on or ignored and he didn't want to do that with anyone.

Tony knew in his heart that he would only be satisfied with one girl and that was Janessa. Her boy friend Bradley, had gone off to college and would only be back occasionally. Janessa had a best girl friend named Rose. They had known each other since they began grade school. Rose and Janessa talked about everything. Rose had an older boy friend their Junior year also. Her boy friend and Bradley happened to be best friends too. The two couples spent a lot of time together. Tony and Rose were also friends and had several classes together as Juniors. She was very nice and also very pretty. Tony and Janessa again were in a Government class together as Seniors. The banter between them continued and they both enjoyed it. They were assigned a class project that they would have to work on together outside of class time. After football practice, Tony would drive over to Janessa's house. She and her parents, younger sister and brother didn't live in Butchertown. They lived in what was called Visitation Valley located about four miles South of Butchertown. They had what was called a set of Encyclopedias that contained information about all kinds of topics. It was like the internet, only it was written in volumes. While working on the project Mrs. Kapas provided dinner for them. They would sit at the dinning room table with the encyclopedias and look up information and take notes for their final project. They would work for several hours then head over to Mooney's Ice Cream Parlor and Candy Shop on the corner of Third Street and LaSalle in Butchertown. Mooney's was a very popular place for young people to go to visit. When you walked in the bell on the door rang and you could smell the sweet odor of Ice Cream and the sugar smell of the homemade candy.

Tony opened the door for Janessa as she walked in ahead of him.

" Thank you Tony. " as she looked him right in his eyes

" You better open things for me" she had a little smirk that Tony just loved

"Next time you should open it for me!" Tony tilted his head a little sideways and smiled. She punched him in his shoulder playfully and they laughed.

It had red padded bar stools that could spin 360 degrees that sat usually facing a counter with a full length mirror. It also had wooden booths for four, with the same red padded seats. In the background Mr. Mooney provided music of the old country fair style. Not very loud but it helped with generating a happy atmosphere. It wasn't an official date, but it was just the two of them and it was exciting. They both looked forward to that part of the night.

"What do you want?" Tony asked, as Janessa sat in one of the booths.

"How about a couple of scoops of Rocky Road please.!"

"Nope!" Tony stared at Janessa

"Why not? She was puzzled

"Cause that's what I'm getting! There was a pause as the looked at each other and both laughed.

"Smart al lick"

Tony returned with the bowl of Rocky Road for Janessa and a bowl of two scoops of vanilla with a caramel syrup.

"That looks interesting. Maybe we should share." Janessa reached across the table with her spoon and grabbed a bite.

The project took four nights of working together. The fifth night they put it together so that they could turn it in to the teacher early.

The next Monday at school, Janessa invited Tony over to the house again for dinner on Wednesday night. After dinner, Tony, Janessa and John, Janessa's father , sat in the living room and talked about football. Her father was a big football fan. He watched all of the high school games and attended college games at Kezar Stadium on the weekends. Pro Football did not have a team in San Francisco, but soon would. John gave Tony "a couple of bucks" so that he and Janessa could go to Mooneys for some ice cream..

When he got Janessa home, they stood on the front porch and talked for a few minutes. Tony was about to say good buy, he looked down into her dark eyes. They seemed to twinkle and she made a smurkish smile with her lips. Tony bent down. Their eyes locked as Janessa looked up and their lips gently touched. She happened to be wearing a long nice cowhide coat that gave off an aroma that he would never forget. Every time in the future that he would smell that odor, he would be reminded of this first kiss. His mind was not sure about all of this, but it was the most enjoyable thing that he had ever felt. He wasn't sure what Janessa was thinking, but

Tony almost could not believe what was happening. They pulled back from the gentle kiss, to what seemed like to catch their breath. Then they kissed again,. This time wrapping their arms around each other. They finally said good night.. Tony got into his car for the drive home and watched Janessa wave to him with a beautiful smile and he waved back thinking how unbelievable that that had just happened. As she closed the door behind her and went inside the house.

"Holy Shit" Tony said to himself as he drove home. Tony knew that he would never forget his first kiss!

CHAPTER THREE

Dug in now, with the heat of the day and sweat dripping from his nose, First Sargent Anthony Rucker was able to avoid the bullet fire coming down from the Japanese soldiers positioned in bunkers made of sand bags,large rocks and cement above him . Sargent Rucker hand signaled the remaining Marine Raiders as they settled in. They would wait until it got dark before they started their mission.

This group of men had been selected from their boot camp battalions as the best. Tony, Rich and Joe Dole (Cho) had volunteered for a lengthy thirteen week additional boot camp. They had become very close friends during boot camp. Rich, who called himself "The Duke" came from the little mill town of Bend Oregon. Joe was born and raised on the Dole pineapple plantation on Maui. Because he was raised on the plantation, he was given the last name of Dole. Just like everyone else who worked there. His real last name was Cho.

The training they received was supposed to instill what the Marines called a "closed off and exclusive society". They thought that by isolating soldiers from society and making them believe that they suffered more than any other group, could become a valuable tool. Adding a lack of reward and increasing expectations compared to ordinary men creates a powerful bonding experience. The harsh training and constant reminder that the soldiers volunteered for this training instilled a desire to endure the worst with the possibility to achieve the impossible so that they could prove that it could be done. This group of Raiders would become loyal patriots, but also loyal to each other at a different level and with a greater meaning. They called it a brotherhood. Their bond was the knowledge that they were the elite of the elite and that they had suffered together and endured more than any other fighting force. They could not and would not be defeated.

Their training consisted an emphasis on night combat training that included the ability to do two seventy mile hikes with full gear. It also included hours of physical fitness. The Raiders became experts with all weapons, explosives,land navigation and map analysis. They also became proficient at knife fighting and survival hand to hand fighting. The Raiders were issued and carried two types of knives. The first was the classic Bowie style knife that had a nine inch blade for field craft tasks . The second knife was the Raider Stiletto. It was strictly used as a close quarter stabbing and silting weapon. All of the Raiders became deadly at the art of knife fighting. The Duke, Cho and Rucker were very close. They trusted others, but they had a special Bond. Joe was the shortest, strongest and had a mean streak. Rich was what most people would call a character. He gave everyone a nick name and could keep things fun.

First Lieutenant Michael Erb , who was under orders from the field grade officer Major James Rubio, had ordered First Sargent Rucker to the command center of the 5th Marine Division to meet with him.

The 5th Marine Command Center was five miles East from the coastal town of Naha. With no threat form the Japanese from the air or from long range artillery, The Marines were close to the front. They made camp close to the highway, so that they would be able to get supplies in easily and evacuate the wounded without consequences from the Japanese. It was also on high ground to avoid flooding when and if the rains came. The center itself was located in large tents to keep the sun and rain away from the radio set ups and maps that were spread out on large tables. The tents were broken up to give several operations rooms to set up. The smoke from cigarettes was thick and the dirt floor was a little uneven. Tony could even smell the body odor of all of the Marines through the smell of the smoke. It wasn't a pleasant place to be. Major Rubio was in the center of it all, but several Captains and their staffs had areas around the Majors. The U.S. Army 96th Infantry Division also set up a Center close to the Marines.

"First Sargent Rucker, I want you to take a look at our position on the map and of the Shuri Ridge."

While saluting to Lieutenant Erb, Anthony said" Yes

Sir. What have we got?"

Pointing at a position on a map Lieutenant Erb looked at Anthony and said"I want you to take your platoon of Raiders on a recon mission this afternoon right here." He was pointing to several lines on the map that indicated a small hill seven miles form the center.

"We believe the enemy has several strong holds in and around the Shuri Ridge" Again pointing to the map.

"We... you, need to help us find them. Mark their coordinates and report back to us ASAP. You will not have any cover the last 100 or so meters. You and your men will have to take evasive running patterns to reach the base of the hill. You will start your recon once it gets dark."

"Questions Rucker?"

"When do we leave and when must we return by?"

"The 382ed and 383ed will begin a major movement in 36 hours. So, be back in 30. You have 15 minutes before you move out."

Tony and his platoon had been on several of these missions before. Two on Guadalcanal and one on Iwo Jima.

"Got it Sir" as he saluted.

"Good hunting Sargent" as Lieutenant Erb saluted back.

Anthony gathered his platoon of nine others.

"You got ten to crap and piss and another five to gather rations for 30 hours. Pack as lite as you can."

Rich Scrivner, Tony's best buddy in the Raiders since the first boot camp asked

"How far are we hiking?"

"Seven miles to our starting point. I'll fill everyone in before we hit the trail. Let's take care of business."

Tony gathered his men again before leaving and filled them in.

"We've done this before. Recon assignment. We'll go by two's and split up once we reach the base of this hill." Tony had his map out and pointed to where they were going.

"Make sure you have your maps, so you can mark what you find. Set your watches. We have to be back in 30 hours. Duke, you'll be with me. After reaching the base of the hill we'll wait until dark. Any body got any questions?"

With no questions, the remaining eight paired up as Tony said

"Lets move out men."

"Duke " Anthony pointed to himself.

Tony lead the way, as they went by two's with several

yards apart between them. Not knowing much about the area in which they hiked, they stayed alert along a tree line while staying hunched and didn't talk.

CHAPTER FOUR

As Sargent Anthony Rucker began his hike along the tree line with his platoon he caught a whiff from his cowhide leather strap holding his BAR. It immediately flashed him back to the memory of his first kiss with Janessa. That odor always sent him there. He also remembered the next morning when he picked up his best friend Mike Brodeur for school .

Mike opened the passenger side door of Tony's 1930 black Ford Model T. The nine year old Ford had a

177 cubic inch four cylinder "three speed" engine With two forward gears and one for reverse, the twenty horse power car could reach a top speed of 40 miles per hour.

"Whats up Ruck?"

Mike Brodeur had lived on Kirkwood Avenue across

the street from Tony for as long as they both could remember. Being only a few months older than Tony, Mike looked much older. Sporting long black sideburns to match his mustache and hair, Mike stood five feet nine inches tall and weighed well over 210 pounds. He would say that he was "big boned". Tony and Mike went to Bayview Elementary School from the first grade until they started high school. Mike had played football with Tony all of the way through high school. He also played baseball, which was his first love. It wasn't very often that you ever saw either one without the other. They were closer than brothers. They never told each other any secrets because they always knew what each other was thinking. Some times it was just the way one looked that would give things away.

"Not much, should be a good rest of the week. Finished my social studies project on Monday night, light practice today and beat Balboa on Friday afternoon."

"I figured you would come by last night after dinner, but your car was gone until late."

Tony, Mike, Hannon, Willy and Ross always showed up at Mike's house after dinner time. It was walking distances to everyone and his parents loved having all of the boys at there house. It was a two story home with almost everything upstairs. The basement had a full bar and a very nice stereo that the boys sat around and listened to the latest music. This is when they talked about all of the things guys talk about when girls and parents are not around. They laughed a lot.

As Tony shifted into second gear heading up Third Street towards the school.

"Yeah, Janessa invited me over for dinner and we B.S. ed with her dad about football."

"That all?" Mike asked with a half smile

"Ah, we went to Mooney's for some ice cream."

Mike didn't say anything, he just stared at Tony. A little smile began to creep on to Tony's face

"What?" Tony kinda half laughed.

"That's a shit eat'en grin you got!"

After a short pause Mike continued

"Ruck!! You Son of a Bitch !!!"

"What?"

"You two had more than just a little ice cream."

"Well...yes we did .... and it was awesome."

Tony only knew what the love a son had for a mother was and what the love a son had for a father felt like. What he felt for Janessa was nothing like that. He was excited to be next to her, to hold her. Her smile and smirk was beautiful and made him want to smile. Around her he felt like he had a permanent smile on his face. She made it difficult to think about anything else but her. The way her body's aroma affected his sense of smell also aroused some deep feelings.

Nothing else really seemed to be important. This feeling scared Tony.

What if she didn't have those same thoughts about him? Was he just filling a void in her life? This whole relationship was like a dream. Sometimes good, sometimes not so good.

Their relationship continued on for the next two weeks. Tony had never been on a real date before he became involved with Janessa. He was really nervous when he asked her to the Homecoming Dance at School. To his relief, she quickly accepted and they enjoyed an enchanting evening.

Janessa looked like a princess when he picked her up at her house. He kept thinking how lucky he was to escort her to the dance. She wore her hair up like the women used to do in the twenties. The light color and material of her dress was a perfect compliment to her darker complexion. Her eyes had a sparkle of someone who was excited!

The Homecoming dance, which was in the schools cafeteria, played the music made popular by The Glenn Miller Band. Tunes like; In the Mood, Tuxedo Junction and Moonlite Serenade put the students in a party atmosphere. Other music played was ; Beer Barrel Polka, Billy Holidays "Strange Fruit", "When You wish Upon a Star" by Cliff Edwards and "I'll Never Smile Again" sung by Frank Sinatra. Everyone had a fantastic time. Mike had a date as did Ross and Hannon. They all went to dinner together at a nice restaurant. Tony and Janessa had the most fun of all the four couples.

After the dance and a small bowl of ice cream at

Mooney's, he returned Essa home. Essa sat next to Tony in the front seat of the Ford and just talked for an hour while sitting in front of her house. Finally Tony kissed her.

"I think I should walk you to the front door before your dad comes out."

"Your probably right! "

They stood by the front door for awhile. "I really don't want this night to end Tony."

"I feel the same way."

"Well, we finally agree on something at last." She said with a very big smile. And they both laughed.

They eventually embraced with a long passionate kiss and said "Good night."

The next Friday night after the final football game of the season, the couple went to the Bayview Theater on 3ed and Quesada. The movie that night was "The Shop Around the Corner" staring Margaret Sullivan and James Stewart. Essa and her parents lived South of the theater off of Paul Avenue. As usual, they went to Mooney's Candy and Ice Cream Parlor on the corner of 3ed and LaSalle. They both agreed that it was a fun movie to watch. They sat in the old Ford in her driveway for a while before Tony walked Janessa to her porch. Again they enjoyed a passionate kiss, a smile and a wave good bye.

That week at school went as usual except that

football practice was done and basketball season was starting. Essa was going to be on the Winter cheer leading squad and Tony had a chance at being a starter on the hoop team.

With no games scheduled for Friday night, Tony asked Janessa if she'd like to watch the new Disney movie Pinocchio at the Bayview Theater..

"Ah ... Tony, I'm sorry I can't." She wasn't even looking at him and seemed indifferent.

"OK" Tony replied

"What's up?"

"Tony... Brad is coming home for Christmas break and he'd like to get together that weekend."

Brad had been Janessa's boy friend from the last school year. He had been off to college, where he was playing freshmen football.

"I see. Well.... you guys have a great time. Call me when you are available."

"Tony. It's not like that."

"What is it like ?" Tony waved with a smile and walked away. He wasn't sure if he was mad, disappointed or both. He knew he wasn't very happy.

School and especially the class that they were in together, were difficult on both and filled with tension. They did exchange hello's but that was it. Both of them and their situation, were the talk of the older kids at school. Tony was not going to let that seem to bother him as he went about his business.

"So whats up with you and Essa? Mike asked on the way to school.

"I'm not really sure. Brad came home for break and she wants to see him."

Mike answered "He'll be gone in a few weeks and things can get back the way they were."

"Not sure it will. I guess we'll see. More important, how do you like being the manager?

Mike wasn't playing basketball but instead he was going to be the manager.

"Piece of cake. Coach Johnson really only needs me for some things during practice and I'll do some stats for him on game night. The bonus is, I get to travel with the team!"

Also on the basketball team were Mike and Tony's other real good friends. Sean Hannon and Rob

Silver were the two best players. They went to different grade schools and middle schools than Mike and Tony went to but had found there way together through classes and mutual interests and personalities. Jimmy Ross lived on the corner of LaSalle and Mendell. It was just around the corner from Kirkwood and was also part of the team. Jim had gone to catholic schools the whole time but decided that he would join all of his friends at Commerce for his Senior year. He was also a really good baseball player and he fit right in with the others.

Commerce High School had a home basketball game on Friday night. Mike and Tony went to Mooneys after the game along with many other players, cheerleaders and students. Janessa wasn't one of them.

While sitting in one of the booths that faced the long counter and huge mirror, Tony and Mike sat across from Debbie and Susan. They were both part of the cheerleading squad and had been friends with the two guys since they meet at Bayview Elementary School.

"You know Tony, Janessa was just using you until Brad came home. " Debbie said as she ate a bite of Rocky Road ice cream.

"Thanks for sharing Deb. Way to make old Tony feel good about himself."

"Well Mike, its true! We all know it. You two just didn't want to see it."

"Thanks everyone for the confidence boost. I'll be just fine". Tony spooned up some vanilla ice cream with strawberries on it.

Those comments gave Tony a lot to think about that night and the next few days. Saturday night Mike and Tony went to a party and dance at "The Corral" which was located behind the Bayview Athletic fields on Kirkwood. It was walking distance from the their homes, but Tony drove Mike anyway. The Corral was a gathering place for people of all ages in Butchertown. In the day time it was a place to ride horses and practice rodeo skills. It used to be a place where people kept their horses. Because streets were now paved, there wasn't much use or reason to own the once noble animal.

Mike and Tony brought along a bottle of bourbon that Tony took from his fathers stash. His father drank only on special occasions and had quite a few bottles that were given to him on each Christmas from his costumers. He would not miss one bottle.

"Dam...That's nasty stuff" Tony shook his head and winched as he handed the bottle to Mike.

"It will taste better on the third or fourth pull"

Yeah... I know, but but maybe we should mix it with something?"

Mike took a long pull, wiped his mouth with his sleeve across his mouth "No need too!"

There were many young people there and the boys were having a good time. They had finished the fifth of bourbon and were feeling no pain.

Hannon and Ross were there with their usual flair. They were giving all of the pretty girls a chance on the dance floor. They too had a bottle of spirits and were also feeling no pain. Silver was also there. But he spent all of his time with his cheerleading girl friend Michelle.

Tony danced with several of his long time friends and classmates when one particular girl, who happened to be one year younger than Tony, began to make sure all of his time was her's.

As he was relieving himself behind the stacks of hay for the few horses that remained at the corral, Mike walked up next to him and began to do the same thing.

"So... Wendy's kinda got your eyes tonight."

"Yep. Why not! I've been thinking about what Deb and Susan said last night about Janessa using me. I think I should give some of the girls around here a chance to change my mind about Essa."

"I agree, but be careful."

"Sure thing but it's time for this guy (pointing his thumb at his chest) to widen his options." Both Mike and Tony laughed and walked back to the dance area.

Tony ended up walking Wendy over to the Hill Top Park and spending time with her under a big oak tree.

Monday at school, Janessa walked up to Tony and punched his shoulder. It wasn't the usual playful hit.

"What's that for?" Tony was surprised by how hard she hit him and almost made him mad.

"Wendy huh!" Janessa wasn't happy either.

"Yep! Wendy it was. She doesn't have a boyfriend like someone I know."

"That's not fair!!" Essa responded

"You are right...as usual"

"Tony, don't be that way."

"What way is that? It's ok for you to be with Brad, but not for me to be with whom ever."

The next few weeks were tension filled between Tony and Janessa. Tony made sure he was seen with other girls not only at school but around town. Everything got back to Essa. Not much was said

between the two. Tony did miss being around her and really wanted to get back to the way things had once been. He didn't even let Mike know what he was thinking. He wanted people to think nothing bothered him. The other girls really didn't mean anything to him. They were just a way to hurt Janessa, just like she had hurt him.

Basketball would soon move into January and the team was playing well. Tony had made the starting lineup. He didn't score much, but he didn't need to. The team had several players capable of scoring Everyone was on the bus going to the next game across town to Mission High School. Mike, who was a very popular person with all of the players as well as the cheerleaders, was sitting in the back of the bus telling jokes and stories. Jim and Sean were always knee deep in the goings on. Silver was close but usually sat with his girl friend.

Tony was sitting alone towards the middle, when the cheerleaders got on the bus. Janessa walked right to where he was sitting and sat right next to him. She was so close, she bumped him.

"We need to talk!." she said

"Really ... before the game?'

"Yes.. It's important."

"I guess your going to tell me what ever your thinking, no matter what!"

Janessa went on to explain that she really missed being around Tony. That she was hurt by his actions with the other girls but she couldn't blame him. She also explained that she was confused about her relationships with Brad and Tony. She knew that he was seeing other girls at college and that hurt her too.

"It really doesn't concern me what Brad does. Only what you do Essa."

Tony went on. "I miss being around you. You make me happy, but lately you have also hurt me."

"Tony.. we need to stop doing this to each other."

"That would be nice." Tony smiled

"Promise me that you will go out with me on News Years Eve. It's next week."

Tony and Janessa brought in the new year of 1939 with a picnic of sorts at Coit Tower. Coit Tower over looks the City of San Francisco. It sits on what is called Nob Hill in the Italian section of town. It is at the end of a dead end road that winds up a hill.

They took the staircase to the top of the lighted tower and open air balcony. That's were they ate their picnic and talked and kissed for several hours. It was a night that neither one would ever forget.

CHAPTER FIVE

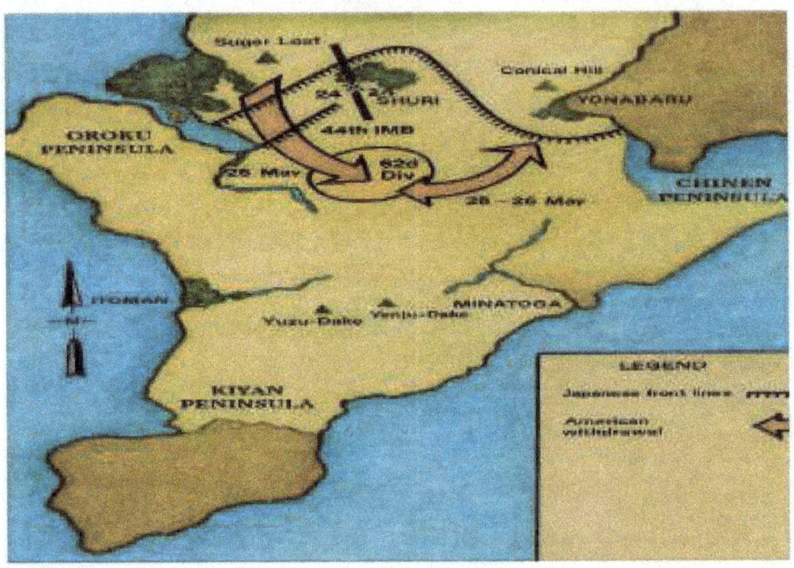

First Sargent Anthony Rucker joined PFC Pete Pardini and Corporal Wilfred Simpson as they made their way to the side of the hill and out of site from the Japanese. Anthony had placed Rich's rifle in the ground and his helmet on top of it to mark the fallen soldier. Someone from the US Army would later take good care of it. Anthony felt horrible about the loss of his closest friend in the Raiders. They had been together since the first day of Boot camp. Anthony also knew that you got ta do what you got a do, so that you can do what you want to do. It was time to get on and finish the mission.

Dark had set in as they slowly approached what seemed like a gathering of the enemy force that was well hidden. They each had extensive map training, so they could easily figure coordinates of the enemies position. After watching the encampment, they figured out that it was an artillery outfit. The Japanese had placed a well hidden .47 MM anti tank gun in the side of the hill. It was on what looked like train tracks as it could be moved in and out of the cave with ease. Making sure they each made notations of the location on their own maps before they moved on. This ensured that the information would make it back to the command center.

For the next 24 hours, they circled the area noting locations of bunkers, mortar positions and land mine fields. Just before sunrise, on their return, PFC Pardini came face to face with a surprised Japanese soldier. This sleepy sentry, yelled out to two of his fellow soldiers. On there way to help their fellow sentry, Tony and Wilford intercepted them. With Stiletto's in hand they tackled the running Japanese. Quietly and quickly , they covered their mouths with one hand and slid their knives across the wind pipes of the two Japanese soldiers. At the same time. Pete flicked his knife with an under handed throw to the neck of the man he was facing. All three acts took silent seconds and accomplished the end of the brief skirmish.

First Sargent Anthony Rucker, as well as all of the Marine raiders in his platoon, had become real good at killing in hand to hand situations. The training that prepared them for this type of situation had come in quite handy. On Guadalcanal Anthony had experienced his first close encounter kill. Having looked into the mans eyes as they both battled for their lives, those eyes continually came back to haunt him at nights. Shooting someone from a distance was way different than killing with your hands. That night, Anthony had taken several lives during close quarter fights. He experienced the same thing on the Island of Iwo Jima. It's what he had trained for, but it still made him sick. It was war. Him or them. The band of brothers fought for each other. They must all return and complete their mission. Killing became second nature to most of them. Anthony did not enjoy it, he thought some of the men in his platoon did. Those eyes! He made sure after that, he would never look his enemy in the eyes.

First Sargent Rucker could not tell someone how many men he has killed, just that it was a lot. He justified it by thinking it was for the greater good and for freedom. He couldn't think that those men might have been part of families or had a wife and children. He was saving the lives of other U.S. Soldiers. And he was. He still fought in his mind a conflict of his up bringing. Raised a practicing Catholic, killing was wrong and he would have to find a priest before he died, so that he could confess his sins. He could not wait for this war to be over.

Anthony, Pete and Wilfred returned to the command post on April 4th 1945. Of the ten riders who left, seven returned with valuable information. The U.S. 96th Infantry Division had advanced early that morning before the Raiders return. They moved along Okinawa's Highway 1. As they approached the hill, they took heavy fire from the ridges on their East side. Three medium tanks from the 763 ed tank Battalion took hits from the .47 MM anti tank guns Anthony, Pete and Wilfred had discovered. Being well concealed, the U.S. didn't know where to return fire. All three tanks were destroyed. The U.S. attack was forced to retreat.

On the morning of April 5th, with the info that the Raiders came back with, the USS Tennessee started heavy fire on the Japanese positions. Using 14/50 main battery guns the USS Tennessee took out one of the .47 MM anti tank guns, mortar positions, hidden bunkers and some mine fields. The Tennessee pounded the area for an hour, but could not completely destroy all of the enemies strong holds.

Later on that afternoon, the 383 Infantry Regiment moved out towards Cactus Ridge, which was part of what was called the Shuri Line. It was slow moving forward for the U.S. Forces. The open area still had mines that were active. One .47 MM anti tank gun was still protected by the cave in the ridge. It was still able to fire on the open field and any tanks that could make it to the open area. The system of caves on Cactus Ridge was so well protected and camouflaged that this was going to be a difficult operation.

During that afternoons battle, the 383 gained only 1,300 yards. When the tanks and men had tried to pass through a gap in a minefield, the .47 MM gun hit two tanks that had to be abandoned. The Americans took many casualties and were forced to withdraw under the heavy Japanese machine gun, rife and mortar fire.

Anthony's platoon of Marine raiders had taken part in the frontal assault and had also joined the withdrawal.

"Make a hole and get in it. We'll be here for awhile." Anthony ordered his platoon after they had fallen back.

"I'll check with Lieutenant Erb on what comes next.

Get some water and any food you can."

Anthony made his way back to the command center. Lieutenant Erb was still in the field, so Anthony approached Major Rubio.

Major Rubio was a tall Mexican American that was a graduate of the Navel Academy at Annapolis. He looked tired and had not shaved in a day or two. Not wearing any kind of hat and smoking a chewed on cigar, Major Rubio signaled by waving at Anthony to continue over to him.

"First Sargent Rucker!"

"Sir" Both saluted

"Sargent we have a big problem on that Ridge! Lieutenant Erb stated that you know right where that .47 MM is."

"Yes Sir I do."

"The Tennessee's bombardment can't penetrate the cave that protects it. The Japs must be repairing the tracks after we hit them to keep that gun operable. " The major said all of this without taking his cigar out of his mouth. It bounced as he talked and the smoke went right into his eyes. Rubio paused and looked at Anthony.

"After dark hits tonight, take your men and take that gun out."

"At all cost Sir?"

"Take what ever you need. We don't need prisoners. Fight until the last man. No one comes back until that gun is destroyed. Understand!"

"Yes Sir." They both saluted and as Anthony turned to leave.

"Rucker!" Major Rubio called out.

"Sir?"

"Good Luck!"

Anthony gathered his platoon of 13 Raiders. He took six from another platoon to give him the numbers he thought that he needed. All of these Raiders had a lot of experience and were well versed in night fighting. They were good and confident in their skills and each other.

They carried only what they would need. Nothing extra. Two of the raiders carried only motors and amo for them. Others carried either a BAR or a Thompson machine gun. They all had extra grenades and of course their knives. Corporal Simpson was going to set the explosive charges in the cave.

"Pardini and I will lead two groups. My group will approach from the East flank and Pardini will be on the West flank."

Anthony then looked at Simpson. "You'll be with me.

You and I will find our way to the cave and blow it. If I remember , there are some big boulders next to the opening that we can use for cover."

Anthony looked at the rest of the Raiders and gave the final command "I'll fire the first shot. That should give Simpson and I a diversion to get to the cave from the boulders. If it doesn't blow after ten minutes, Mahale and Webber you will be next . We'll keep trying until the last man."

"Any questions?"

They started to move into position while it became dark. The night would provide extra cover. After thirty minutes of winding through heavy brush and trees. They moved to their flanking positions. Anthony and Simpson spent the last part of their assault on their bellies crawling to the boulders They found a spot about ten feet from the cave opening. The two groups had time to set their mortars up and readied their machine guns for the diversion fire.

Anthony looked at Simpson " You ready?"

"Now is as good as any. Lets do it."

Anthony raised his BAR and took down one of the sentries standing guard. Pardini took down another sentry as the others opened fire on the bunker that was out in front of the cave. A handful of Japanese soldiers ran out of the cave and took positions around the cave while Anthony and Simpson ducked in behind them and into the cave. Two mortar shells landed on the tracks and in the bunker. The Japanese seemed to be confused by the attack and where the fire was coming from. That distraction helped Anthony and Simpson reach the 47MM gun which was back inside the cave sitting on the rail tracks. Simpson began to set the explosives as Anthony stood guard. Anthony held his 45 pistol ready to shoot. It was more accurate at close range and easier to fire. It was a good thing Anthony was ready. He took down two enemy soldiers while Simpson continued to work.

"Done! Lets beat it."

Simpson started to unwind the cable attached to the explosives as they both made their way out of the cave. The gun fire and explosions from out side the cave had continued as they finally reached the boulders for cover.

"Let 'er rip!" Anthony shouted out to Simpson.

Simpson pushed down on the firing mechanism. The sound from the explosion was deafening. Rock, smoke, debris and parts of metal came flying out of the cave. All of that momentarily stopped the shooting. Anthony and Simpson quickly made their way into the bush on their bellies. The Raiders kept up the fire on the cave and the surrounding area to give Rucker and Simpson time to get away from the cave.

Each of the flanking Marine attack groups adjusted the angle of the mortars to explode at the mouth of the cave. They placed several shells to that spot and then began their retreat. Taking turns protecting their rear, the Marines made their way out of the brush and trees to a gathering point.

Of the 13 Marines who started the mission, all finally made it back together before heading to camp and the command area. Although they were all alive, many were wounded in some capacity. First Sargent Anthony Rucker sat in the make shift infirmary with his wounded comrades. Fortunately for Anthony, the bullet that hit him on his way out of the cave, went completely through his upper left arm without hitting any bone. It hurt, but he was going to be fine. He actually could flex his arm at the elbow. Some how some one produced a gallon jug of homemade moonshine. Some one in the Cee Bee's camp had set up a still. They were always left without any field grade officers to watch over them. The first few swigs tasted horrible, but it had a major kick to it and it helped relieve some of the pain from the injuries.

Major Rubio came in to check on the 13 Marines under his command. He carried a large box of cigars and passed them out.

"Here you guys go! Nice work taking out that 47 MM cannon. The 383ed division lead by our tanks broke through that opening in the barbed wire fence."

PFC Pardini, while holding the jug and an unlit cigar in his mouth. "What's next Major?"

"Defiantly not done yet. We've secured Cactus Ridge, but Kakazu Ridge will be hell. They're dug in a maze of deep caves. It's going to have to be yard by yard. You guys get better. We are going to need those of you that can continue."

During the next five days, the Marine 1st Division remained at an area away from the fighting on Kakazu Ridge. The U.S. Army's 382ed and 383ed infantry took up the assault on the Ridge.

Anthony and the Raiders took advantage of the five days. They showered, washed clothes, caught up on sleep, ate and cleaned their weapons. They even had a chance to play some poker and laugh a little. The whole time they could hear the battle going on and knew they would be back to it soon.

Taking advantage of the time away from the fighting, Tony wrote a letter home to his parents. He couldn't tell them much, other than that he was fine and looking forward to the end of the war.

Dearest Mother and Father,

I hope you two are doing fine. I hear that the war has had it's affect on food and gas supplies. I'm sure its affected you in other ways. Just know that your sacrifices are helping us fight this horrible war.

I can't wait to get out of this hell hole they call the beautiful South Pacific. I don't think I will ever come back . I can't tell you too much about where we are and what I'm doing. I just want to let you know that I'm all in one piece! A few aches and pains but you should know that the training we received has proven to be very good. We are prepared for almost everything. We have plenty to eat and we do get time to sleep and rest.

What we are doing is for a great cause and I am glad that I went into the Marines. We are the best. I miss being home! I don't think the enemy can last much longer. They fight hard, but so do our boys and we have many.

I'll be home soon.

With Much Love,
Your Son, Anthony

Anthony hoped the letter would put his parents at some ease. He didn't want to let them know how fierce the fighting was. He would never tell them about the hand to hand combat and that he actually killed anyone. What they didn't know would not hurt them. He wanted them to think that he slept well at nights.

Tony's mother, Edith, had to read the letter out loud to Tony's father James, or as his friends called him, Jimmy. Jimmy was always misplacing his glasses. He worked at Union Tallow Works which was on the corner of Evens Ave and Keith. Being six blocks away, Union Tallow was walking distance from there home. Jimmy had been working there since he had graduated from Commerce High School in 1916. He had done several jobs at Union after beginning as a fat grinder. At the age of 40, Jimmy had become the foreman of the tallow company. He was hoping that he would be able to stay on as the foreman when Allens Meats, which was located just up the street on Evens, bought Union Tallow Works. The sale would become final any time now.

Jimmy had met Edith at Commerce when she was a sophomore and were married after she graduated in 1918. They had been living on Kirkland ever since. Following Tony's birth in 1921,William, Edward and Judy.

One of the other ways that the Raiders passed time was to play craps. Someone always had a set of dice. They made sure the stakes were low, usually smokes. No one had any money. Anthony's mind often wondered back to his home in The City during those games and down time. With his experiences at DeNikes back home, he did really well at those crap games. Cyril DeNike had taught Mike and Tony how to play dice! Although he didn't smoke , he used the smokes to trade for other things.

CHAPTER SIX

After Tony and Essa spent the wonderful evening at Coit Tower, things began to get back to the way they both liked it. The way it was when the school year had started.

Brad had returned to his school and it was just Tony and Essa. They did things with others, even though he knew that many were thinking Essa was using him again. But it felt pretty good get' en used. With so many basketball games, time on the bus together and school, the days were going by fast. Tony was not seeing other girls as long as Essa had time for him.

Although Mike was Tony's best friend, they didn't talk

about personnel things. That's what girls did. Tony, as well as Mike, like to keep certain things, like their feelings, future plans and goals, to themselves. Tony wasn't really sure what his feelings, goals and plans were anyway. He didn't think that Mike had any himself! Tony was thinking about going to a college and playing football. He really enjoyed the contact, intensity, comrade re and strategy of the game. School wasn't very exciting to him, but if he wanted to play football, he would have to endure school.

Tony also knew that the more he was around Essa that his feelings grew deeper. He wasn't sure what loving someone romantically felt like, but he was pretty sure he was getting close. Problem was, he wasn't sure what Essa felt about him. They were very young. Too young to get involved at a serious level. He was in a difficult spot with her. They never would share what each other was thinking about the future. He felt at times , she was sending a subtle message to him that he wasn't part of her plans. He didn't think he was sending Essa the same message. He did know that she too, planned to attend college to further her education. Tony felt that he wanted to go somewhere far away. See a different part of the country. That would mean leaving Janessa behind. What was more important? He did know that he had time to figure it out. He also knew that between he and his parents they didn't have the money for him to go to a college or a university. He would have to work at least a year.

Tony and Mike began to hang out at DeNikes Restaurant on the corner of Third and Galvez. Cyril, the owner, knew all of the young kids in the Butchertown neighborhood. He sponsored many baseball teams for the youth in the area along with a Semi Pro baseball team. Tony and Mike had played on some of the teams growing up and got to know Cyril. He was a big man. Always dressed in a suite with a tie and a matching vest. On top of his head was a well placed expensive white cowboy hat. He had gotten his start in the business when he was a teenager. Before the great earthquake and fire that leveled much of San Francisco in 1906, Cyril worked at an establishment on what was called "Irish Hill" just north of Butchertown. Irish Hill was home to four "Hotels" and many wooden shacks that served as homes for many young single men in the area that worked in Butchertown and Hunters Point building ships. A powerhouse located in the area also employed many men. Many of the men were of Irish and Scottish descent.

The four hotels and the Hill were not as popular or talked about as much as the famous Barbary Coast establishments located in the main part of San Francisco. The dance halls on Pacific Street from Montgomery to Stockton, which included places like the Bella Union, The Hippodrome and the most dangerous of all, The Whale. That area of San Francisco was very popular for all of the out of town visitors and those who had extra money.

The area of the Hill near Butchertown included a hotel called The White House. That is were Cyril got his start. He began as a bar back. He was cleaning dishes,mugs, toilets,floors spilled beer, spittoons, vomit and any other odd jobs the bartenders didn't want to do. His boss was a well known Irishman named William Turnbull. Big Bill! Tough as they come. Many tried to take him on, but no one was successful. He lived in a room upstairs at the White House. And was there all of the time. He managed the dance hall, bar, gambling room and the prostitutes. He carried an Irish shalayle that Big Bill didn't mind using on some drunks head.

Cyril began to learn many things from Bill and over the years and put them to good use.

DeNikes was located down the street from all of the slaughter house in Butchertown at the corner of Third and Galvez Ave. It was a popular hang out for all of the workers in the area. It kind of took the place of the Hill. All of the hotels and wooden shacks were destroyed by the fire. The dirt and rocks of the Hill were then used by the City to fill in parts of the bay for construction projects. It had a nice restaurant and bar. It also had a backroom that was used for gambling, but not everyone was allowed and was only used on Saturday nights. Cyril made sure everything was on the up and up. He didn't get a cut out of the gambling. He made his money by selling higher priced alcohol. Also, no prostitutes This helped keep the Police away. Cyril also knew Short the Cop and Big Dick, the two local Cops who patrolled the area. They made sure Cyril knew when they were coming by!

By 1940, the slaughter houses in Butchertown had dwindled down to just four, from the original twenty four that had been rebuilt after the 06 fire.

Tony and Mike had worked at DeNikes as bus boys and part time help since they were ten years old. They lived four blocks away on Kirkwood and could walk to DeNikes.

By the time they were Seniors in high school, Cyril let the boys in the backroom on Saturday nights to help pour drinks and keep the place clean. On a Saturday night in April, Tony and Mike were talking with Cyril about getting full time work when they were done with high school.

"Hey Cyril, you no anybody at Allens that could get us on?"

Allens was the largest of the slaughter houses and also located on Evens Ave just off of Third Street. It went all the way to Kirkwood, which was five city blocks.

"Tony, I know a couple guys. In fact many who work there. I'll put the word out to them for both of you two knuckle heads. You know it will be tough dirty work!"

"Thanks Cyril. Mike and I can handle it. It's just until I can put enough money away to pay for college."

"That's what they all say. Once you start there, you'll be there for ever!

Cyril knew what he was talking about. The jobs were difficult, but they paid good wages. Enough to support a family and live a good life. There weren't that many of those jobs in The City.

Eventually both Tony and Mike were hired at Allens. Cyril had come through again for the boys. Neither one of them had any butchering skills, so they started on the clean up crews. Tony worked the day shift and Mike began on the swing shift.

Most of Tony's work day was spent cleaning up the kill floor while the processing went on around him. He would also work in the holding pens herding the hogs,lambs and cattle to the areas upstairs where the kill floor was. The worst job was getting the hair off of the hogs after they were slaughtered. This was done by scraping the hogs with rosin rocks. What a mess and very strenuous. The beginning workers always stated scrapping the hogs. If you could handle that job, you were considered OK. They went through many would be workers. Tony, though knew that if it was like a test, so he just gutted it out and didn't complain. Tony's day started with the hog kill and the lamb kill. The afternoon ended with the slaughter of the beef cattle.

Working clean up on the hog kill was very messy and difficult. There were times that the hog , while hanging from one leg shackled to a trolley on a rail, would slip off and fall into a pool of the drained blood. People always laugh or joke about trying to grab a hog in a mud filled pen, have no idea on how hard it is to tackle a hog that has been stuck with an eight inch knife, in a pool of its own blood. At least once a week, Tony was tasked to do this very job.

Most of the time Tony spent sweeping up the floor while the hogs were being butchered. They rolled on trolleys hung to the rails above the floor. At the feet where the butchers worked, the old wooden floor was covered with the scraps of fat and often unborn piglets that fell from the open sow bellies. Tony had to dodge the knives as the butchers worked.

At the end of the line, the hogs heads were cut off and dumped in a gondola. Tony got used to looking at the hogs heads with the eyes seeming to stare at him. All of the heads were crawling with maggots. At first, Tony was uneasy looking at them but he got used to that too.

The work on the lamb and beef lines was a lot easier. The noise was much louder. Workers had to yell at each other or use hand signals to communicate. Often times during the beef kill, there wasn't much to do for the clean up crew of one.. So, Tony had to stay busy cleaning up restrooms and the lunchroom. He would also work in the pens and in the coolers pushing beef around after they were in half's.

"Hey easy money! Let's get you working with Red. You need to learn how to use a knife and get some butchering skills."

Jack Federico was the day shift foreman at the plant. He made sure things went as planned. He also placed the men at different stations to keep them learning new jobs and to have flexibility with the workers. Many of the men liked to be able to switch around and break up the monotony of the job. Jack had been watching Tony work as part of the clean up crew and liked what he saw. Hard working, smart and never bitched about the work. Jack Federico was a big man. He had been working in the business for years. He could do any job and had done all of them. He demanded hard work from his guys and only excepted high performance from them. He took no crap from anyone and had been known to take guys outside and settle arguments with his fist. His bald head and half smoked cigar between his teeth made him easy to find!

Red Stevens also had been working at Allens since he graduated from Gallello High School in 1932. Red was the star quarterback for the football team during his Junior and Senior years. He was well liked by everyone and knew his job. He came from a long line of butchers and grew up in the

Butchertown neighborhood.

Tony's nights, Sunday through Thursday, were spent at home, getting to bed early. Friday and Saturday nights were usually spent at Cyril's back room learning how to play dice. Craps was a fun game and both he and Mike were getting pretty good at. The older guys weren't to happy losing their money to a young buck. Because Tony was from the neighborhood and Cyril liked him, the old guys put up with him. Tony and Mike, when he played, both knew to keep their mouths shut and just play. Cyril made sure that they didn't waste their money by buying drinks.

Every once in a while, Tony would call Essa. She was busy too. She worked at her uncles ice cream and candy store out in the Mission District. She too, wanted to attend college and possibly become a school teacher. But like most, money was an issue.

Tony and Essa did get the chance to hit the movie house in October to see "The Shop Around the Corner". James Stewart and Margaret Sullivan were the two stars of the movie. As usual, they had a great time. Afterword they found their way to the Saint Francis Hotel, just across from Union Square. There was a nice lounge that had music and dancing. Glenn Millers Band had made several hits like " In the Mood" and "Tuxedo Junction"popular. Many small bands would play these along with many others. Essa was easy to talk with! She was just so pretty and alluring. She knew how to apply just enough make up to accentuate the shape of her face. Essa turned heads when she walked into a room because of her enchanting walk. Tony knew he was with the most fascinating and nicest girl in any room. Time between them always seemed to go too fast.

Essa was really excited to get back to school. She felt that with a year off working, she could save enough money to get her started. Essa would have to work part time though while attending College. Staying with her parents would also save money. Her relationship with Brad was still an on and off again thing. He really had a hold on her. Tony just didn't want to see other girls. He didn't have the time,money or interest in them.

One thing Tony did know, was that he didn't want to work as a butcher at Allens or any other slaughter house! Even though he got to do several jobs, it just wasn't for him.

The men working there were good guys. The talk at lunch was getting away from sports, like baseball and boxing to what was happening in Europe. The possibility of the United States going to war over seas was getting close. If that was to happen, who would go? Half the workers had families and wondered if they would be drafted.. Tony would for sure get drafted, but he didn't want to be an Army grunt. There had to be something better, different. They all talked about the different branches of service and what they thought they offered. If the United States was to enter into the World War, Tony would be going. More and more he tried to learn about the programs the Marine Corp offered. He also thought that serving in the Pacific would be better than the cold European Theater. Little did he know how soon he would be signing up to be a Marine.

He and Essa had talked some long hours about the future, most of which included him going to war. She knew that Tony would have to. Not being in school, young and not married made him a shoe in to get drafted. She also knew that Brad would be exempt and he wasn't going to volunteer to go to war.

December 7th 1941 changed everything for Tony. On the 8th of December, Tony enlisted in the United States Marine Corp.

CHAPTER SEVEN

With the five days of rest, Tony along with the rest of the Marine 1st division, joined up with the 6th Marines. The two Marine divisions combined with the U.S. Army's 7th,27th,77th and 96th to form what was then called the 10th Army.

After the U.S. Forces took Kakazu Ridge, the Japanese 32ed Army retreated over 30,000 personnel to the Kiyan Peninsula. This area was the southern most tip of Okinawa. It became the home of those soldiers in an area of many rocky hills, small valleys and countless caves. Many of the caves had been dug out to create a massive tunnel system.

The Tenth Army was given the task to go hill to hill, cave by cave and destroy the remaining Japanese Army in what would become the worst fighting in the Pacific Theater.

Between April 6th and the beginning of May, when the tenth Army took control. The fighting continued. The Japanese used Kamikaze attacks from Kyushu. It is the southern most island of the four Japanese islands. Those missions sunk 20 American ships and damaged 157 more. The kamikazes also raised havoc on the U.S. Ground forces on Okinawa.

During the month of April, Tony and his Marine Raiders continued to do recon missions in preparation for the Tenth Army's planned assault on the Kiyan peninsula.

1st Lieutenant Michael Erb gathered his group of 1st Sergeants and Master Gunnery Sergeants.

"Word has come down from the top brass that we are going to move out into the hills. Those piece of shit bastards are tucked away in caves and tunnels. We have to go literally yard by yard and remove the Nips one by one."

Tony looked around at all of his fellow Marines. With already dirty unshaven faces, no one blinked and eye. Many had cigarettes hanging from their mouths as they stared at the Lieutenant waiting for more.

"This is going to be the worst fighting of this fucking war! After this it's on to their home turf. They will die before they surrender. Prepare for this to last a long, long time."

Master Gunnery Sergeant Bishop spoke up.

"1st Lieutenant Erb! When do we move out?"

Gunny Bishop usually called 1st Lieutenant Erb, Mick when no one else was around. They had become good friends and Erb relied on Bishop for a lot of things. Erb replied

"Gunny! As soon as possible. Prepare your men to move out by zero nine hundred. It's Zero eight hundred right now. We will all meet in the staging area. This will most likely be the last time the men will see this place until the operation is over. We may get replacements, but no one is leaving until we kick their ass off this island!"

The fighting continued through the months of April and May with heavy casualties. The extraction of the Japanese soldiers was bloody, very difficult and with close hand to hand fighting. The Japanese often used Okinawan civilians to get them supplies and water. They would also use them as human shields as they moved through and around the Americans. Hundreds of civilians were mistakenly shot by Americans and many more executed by the Japanese. Hundreds also committed suicide by jumping off cliffs.

When May came to an end, the monsoons began. The large amounts of rain and strong winds made things almost impossible. Heavy machinery became useless. What roads that were there became quagmires of mud. The valley floors became running rivers and in some places, little lakes.

Tony and his men had never been in such horrible conditions. They were wet and soaked the entire time. They had ponchos to cover them, but they seemed almost worthless. Because of the horrible conditions, trying to get wounded and dead soldiers out of the area was almost impossible. Japanese snipers were always looking to take out moving soldiers. It didn't matter what time of day, men who were careless would get shot. Tony would wake up each morning and look at the red heart he had tattooed on his left sleeve. Along with the leather strap on his helmet, this was a reminder of Janessa. Just another way to help him get through what was ahead of him.

Many dead Japanese soldiers and civilians laid decaying in the mud and pools of monsoon rain water. At first many of the U.S. Soldiers struggled with the sight of maggots crawling in an out of the dead bodies eyes, ears and mouths. Tony just looked at those sights as if he were back at Allens in the hog kill. He'd seen the maggots every day crawling on the hog heads.

The mud was the kind of mud that sucked the soldiers feet into it. Added to the mud was all of the soldiers urine and feces. Guys just did their business any where they could find a safe place. Much of the time it was close to where they slept and ate. The smell was just as bad as the sight of the maggots. Tony just flashed back to his days in Butchertown and its smells.

All of the men were on edge all of the time. They got very little sleep and the food was bad.

Word came down from commanders to the sergeants to motivate the guys under their command.

Tony had his squad, which was now down to eight from twelve, around him.

"We all feel the same. Cold, hungry,soaked. We all have the shits and who else knows what! If we want to get off of this piece of shit rock they call an island, then we need to get moving and stop feeling sorry for ourselves. We can't be satisfied with the little ground we make each day. Officers want us to get things in gear."

PFC Pardini spoke up.

" What about them? They going to join us in this shit hole? And help out"

"They are in this shit hole right now. And they don't like this anymore than you do. One General has been killed along with other field grade officers. The Japs got to be close to the end!"

Pardini chipped in with" Those fuckers aren't going to surrender! We got to kill' em all."

The kamikaze attacks from Kyuau continued on the fleet off of Okinawa, and continued to raise hell on the ground forces. The 10th Army turned the fighting into a twenty four hour relentless attack on the caves and tunnels. The use of flame throwers helped clearing out those reinforced tunnels. The smell and sight of the burning flesh of not only the Japanese soldiers but also of the Okinawan civilians was difficult to look at. American soldiers would shoot the burning people to stop them from screaming and put them out of their misery.

Instead of measuring their advancement in miles, the 10th and Tony's squad measured it by yards. As the Marine squad of 8, with two replacements, went single file through a small trail up an incline. Tony was second in the line about ten yards behind the point man Corporal Garza. Looking up the hill, Tony saw and felt an explosion. Garza had either stepped on a mine or tripped a Jap booby trap. Garza didn't stand a chance. Tony went flying back down the hill along with rock, debris and parts of Corporal Garza.

When Tony came to, he was lying face down in the mud! His helmet was about five yards away from him on top of a puddle of water and his rife was sticking barrel first in the mud. His head was pounding! The explosion was so loud and powerful it knocked him a good ten yards backwards down the hill. He could see his helmet had a large dent in it from probably a large rock. He also had a large knot on his forehead. For some reason he thought he heard Essa's voice telling him to stay down! Why would she be telling him that? But he finally came to focus and it was Pardini yelling at him.

"Stay down! Stay down!"

Zip ... Zip .. Zip... Tony could hear the machine gun fire and the bullets zipping by his body. The Japs had placed a machine gun nest at the top of the hill and they were firing down on the Marines.

Tony crawled on his belly, just like he had in boot camp. On his belly. But these bullets were live. He crawled past his dented helmet and rifle to cover of a pile of rocks. PFC Pardini was lying down on his belly waiting for Tony.

" I thought you bought it! Pardini said with a tiny smile

" How long was I out?" Tony said as he looked straight ahead at the situation.

"Not long. Maybe a minute or more. I wasn't counting."

"Whats the situation? Tony asked

Garza tripped the explosion. He's probably done. They opened fire from on top of the hill just after the explosion. I got us into two groups of four. One up that side. My group is working up this side. We'll keep em busy with fire, those guys will get close and toss some grenades on em."

It didn't take long before the grenades filled the machine gun nest, and the Japs fell silent.

"We have to stay off those main trails and make our own. I'm sure that most of the easy trails are trapped and or fortified." Tony and his squad had to keep up with the tactics of the Japs. New tactics by the enemy usually cost some lives. Just like Garza's.

After reaching the top of the hill and securing the machine gun nest, The Marines took a few minutes to catch their breath. While the other Marines gathered up what was left of Garza.

"Can I speak freely Gunny?" PFC Pardini had some thoughts he wanted to share with Tony.

"Sure. Whats up?"

"Gunny... How come you are such an asshole?"

"What?" Tony smiled at Pardini but wanted to hear what he had to say. Pardini didn't expect the smile but went on.

"Gunny. You never talk with us about shit other than this war. You drive us hard and never give us anything good. You don't even know our first names. You treat us like shit! Sir!" Pardini went on

"I've been with you since before Iwo. Me, Deloretto and Sully. We don't know anything about you. We know your first name starts with A. That's why we call you Asshole when you aren't around."

Tony responded "That it?"

"That's enough for now Sir!"

"When I was lying face first in the mud, did you want to come and help me?"

"Fuck no!"

"If we were buddies and I called your first name for help, would you come and save me?"

"Probably, yes I would."

"That would have been the dumbest thing you could have done." Tony went on

Instead, what did you do?"

"I organized the rest of us and continued to fight on."

"That's right, that's what a good Marine does."

Tony paused for a second and looked at the PFC

"Since Iwo, I've never heard anyone call my name for help. I never will. Listening to someone cry out your name for help and knowing that you can't. Well, I just don't want to be there." Tony looked Pardini right in the eyes and said

"I ain't your friend, I'm your sergeant. I set the example. I've lost too many Marines that I've been in charge of. If all of those guys were my close friends, I'd be a fuck 'en mess and shitty Marine."

Pardini wasn't sure what to say. He just looked at Tony

You're a good marine PFC. Now put your gear together, and get ready to move on."

Tony Rucker would never forget the sights and sounds from his horrible experience on Okinawa. And neither would those who spent anytime in those battles in the South Pacific. For the rest of his life he would have visions in his sleep that would wake him in pools of cold sweat. Like almost all of those who fought during the occupations of the Pacific Islands, they became reluctant to talk about their experiences and tried to hind them somewhere in the deep parts of their memories.

By June 22ed, the last Japanese fortified underground headquartered cave on a steep hillside was over run by the 1st Marines. Other than an occasional sniper or small groups of Japanese soldiers, the fighting was over. Some of the Japanese soldiers remained hidden among the Okinawan civilians. Eventually, they too were exposed.

Sitting around in a safe dry area Sargent Rucker and what was left of his Marine squad began discussing the future. Tony thought about what PFC Pardini had talked with him about getting close to his men. But he just needed to let his guard down, relax and be a human again.

"Do you know how difficult it's going to be to fight those Nip bastards on their own turf!" Pardini said as he took a long drag on his cigarette followed by a drink from his canteen.

Tony, who was standing with his dented helmet to his left side, rife leaning against his right leg, canteen in his left hand, cigarette cupped in his right hand between his thumb and forefinger.

"We are going to lose many good men. And it will take years. We've been pretty lucky to make it this far. I'm not sure we'll make it to the finish of this.

Another replacement Corporal added

"We gotta come up with something special, different than what were doing now. That final push on that island will be hell."

PFC Billings, also a replacement Marine, chipped in

"I hear we gone to bomb the shit out of 'em. That's what talk was come e'n over here. With these air strips so close, I hope back home can make enough bombs and planes to do the job."

It wasn't long after the final battle took place on Okinawa that the United States took the final steps to end the war in the Pacific with Japan. On August 6th 1945 at 8:15 am, "Little Boy", the bombs nick name, was dropped over the Japanese town of Hiroshima. The Enola Gay, a USAAF B-29 bomber, released the bomb that exploded 1800 feet above the unsuspecting town. Five square miles was reduced to ash. An estimated 120,00 civilian deaths was the result. Three days later "Fat Man" eliminated 73,00 Japanese in the city of Nagasaki.

On August 14th, the United States accepted the unconditional surrender from Japan, with the final signing taking place on September 2ed 1945.

The War was over! Now occupation of Japan and the rebuilding of islands like Okinawa began. The 10th Army, under the leadership of General MacArthur had the task of destroying any and all of Japans war materials. For Tony and his men who spent many long months fighting in those horrible conditions was now over. The memories would stay with all of them until they passed away or took their own lives because of the things that they had done.

CHAPTER EIGHT

Tony and the rest of the men of his platoon of Marines that had combined with the US Army to form the Tenth Army on Okinawa had returned to to San Diego by December of 1945. They were given their Honorable Discharge just before Christmas.

Tony hoped a train heading North. Sitting in the Observation Car, he watched the scenery go by. He hadn't seen this part of his country. All of the farm land, small towns and an occasional large town helped him understand just a little of why he and his fellow soldiers had fought for. He also knew he was tired. Tired of people, orders and fighting. He wanted to go somewhere quiet and calm.

The family was so excited to see Anthony walk through the doors of the old home on Kirkwood. Many friends and family were there to greet him. Hugs were plenty and so was the booze and food. Mike was there with a big ole smile and handshake. Other high school buddies also made sure that they wouldn't miss the reunion. Guys from the basketball team, Rob Silver, Sean Hannon and Jimmy Ross marveled at Tony's appearance. He was twenty pounds heavier but strong looking. His face had a little sadness to it. They could tell he was tired as he tried to smile. He had hoped that Essa would have been there. The thoughts of her while he was over seas had helped him survive. No one mentioned her name or what she was up to.

New Years came around and he bought himself a bottle of red wine, grabbed two glasses and drove his old car to Coit Tower. He thought, just maybe she would also be there. Essa too went to the place where they enjoyed an evening. Hopeful that Tony would return. She waited for two hours and with a small tear in her eye, she left. Tony arrived twenty minutes later. He took the old elevator to the top and opened the bottle. He drank slowly as he watched the lights of the City. It was there that he decided to pack up his stuff and catch the next boat to Hawaii.

He found a small vessel that he could take and work on to cover his passage. The five day voyage was a ruff one but he finally made it. One night in a small hotel on Honolulu, Tony found passage on a fishing boat to the little island of Maui. He had served with Joseph K. Cho on Okinawa. Joe grew up on Maui and worked in the pineapple fields. Joe had told him how peaceful the little island was. During Boot camp, Joe talked a lot about home. Tony had hope that he could find Joe on the island. When they went to Iwo Jima, Joe was placed in a different Company than what Tony and Rich were in. They lost track of where each one was.

Tony spent a few nights sleeping on a beach just south of the peaceful town of Lahaina. After spending all of those days and nights on Okinawa, this was paradise. He found a job working as a bartender in the Pioneer Inn, which was located on the corner of Hotel Street and Wharf Streets. The Lahina harbor was located on the other side of the Wharf. The Inn was a nice two story hotel that looked out over the harbor. He also found a little hut like house with a bedroom and a bathroom to rent. He bought a bike and found his way to work every day and to Shark Pit Beach, where he began to learn how to surf. Because he was not Hawaiian, the locals gave him a cold shoulder. It took awhile, but he began to blend in. His black hair was now long to his shoulders, his skin had turned brown and he always had several days of growth on his face.

Tony absolutely loved the laid back lifestyle of the small island. His diet consisted of locally caught fish. Fresh fruit and locally grown vegetables. Some nights he would BBQ right out on the beach after a day of surfing.

He began to make friends with some of the people that he worked with. Kemo, a rather large Hawaiian, was the chef at the Pioneer Inn's restaurant. His brother Willie, along with Kemo, were the ones who introduced Tony to surfing. Willie too, worked with Kemo in the kitchen. Tony was a very valuable worker at the bar. Tony had worked out a deal that allowed him to stay in a small room next to the bar along with meals, in exchange for his work around the hotel, when not in the bar. What little money he made in the bar, helped buy some extra items. He had mastered the local dialect, which some people call pigeon and was able to talk with and interpret for the white visitors that came to the hotel. Lahina was a vacation place for many rich boaters, who would stay at the hotel while docking their boats in the harbor. It wasn't very often, but there were times drunk young sailors on leave would wonder into the bar.

Tony walked into the Pioneer Inn's front door on his way to the bar to start his evening shift.

"How z It Bra" Tony held up the hang loose sign with his right hand as he smiled to Kemo.

"Ah.. tree howlees in da bar making trouble!"

"sailor boys on leave?"

" I tink so."

Tony continued on into the bar. Before he even walked through the open door, he could hear the loud voices of the three sailors.

Hey old lady! We need another three beers! Pronto!"

Lillian was an older Hawaiian women. She was short and very round and watched over the bar during the afternoons until Tony came in.

"I got this Lill!"

Tony walked slowly around the old wooden bar. It had the old mirror behind it that went the length and several stools that stood in front of it. It still had several old spittoons from the days that visiting whalers and sailors used back in the late 1800's. The bottom of the bar had a copper foot rest that also went the distance of the bar.

"Hey long hair get us some beers!'

Tony reached under the bar and took out a rubber band that he used to fix his hair into a pony tail.

"That's no way to treat a guy trying to make a living!" Tony smiled

Tony then said in a nice calm voice. "You need to be more polite or I'll have to ask you to leave."

Of the three sailors, the smallest one was doing all of the talking.

"Ok buddy! Three beers PLEASE!" He laughed and turned to look at his two friends.

As Tony went to the cooler, Keiba, the young Hawaiian girl who worked at the front desk, walked into the bar to grab some napkins so she could bring them back to the front desk. Tony smiled at Keiba and pulled the three beers from the cooler. He used an opener on the bottles and placed them on the bar.

"Glasses? He asked the sailors

They didn't answer. They grabbed the bottles and headed straight for Keiba and surrounded her.

Keke, as she was called by her friends, was a beautiful 22 year old women. She was taller than the loud mouthed sailor who stood right in front of her. Keke was very athletic looking as she had spent many days on the beach with her brothers Willie and Kemo surfing. Having had two brothers, she was not intimidated by these guys. She, as they say in Hawaii, gave them the "stink eye".

The tallest of the three sailors grabbed her by the arm and said

" You little bitch. Show us some respect."

Before he even finished speaking, Tony was over the top of the bar and right in the middle of things. He grabbed the tall sailors arm and forced him to release Keke.

"You got this all wrong men" Tony stood nose to nose with the big guy.

"Time to leave"

The small sailor grabbed Tony and pulled out a small knife. Tony released his arm and stepped back.

Tony just smiled. It hadn't been that long ago since he had been in situations like this on Okinawa!Standing with his right foot forward and hands on his hips Tony said sarcastically,

"Really? "

The four men faced off and Tony asked again "Really?

That's not a good move on your part"

"I'M GOING TO CUT YOU AND THAT LITTLE BITCH." He held out the knife and took a swipe at Tony.

Instinct took over for Tony. He soon held the knife in his hand and the little sailor was clutching his own throat were Tony had drilled him with a quick punch. The biggest sailor was holding his nose. Tony had placed the bottom of his left hand with a strong and quick punch to the base of the guys nose. Blood began to pour from it. The third sailor just stood there with his hand up.

"I want no part of this."

Keke, had an anger streak in her as well as being beautiful. She poured a pitcher of water over the little guys head and kicked him between the legs. He crumbled to the floor. Lillian circled behind the big sailor and hit him over the head with a full beer bottle. It broke and the beer washed over his face. With all of the noise, Kemo by now had come in from the kitchen along with brother Willie.

"Ah".. He laughed.

"They like meet the ground or what?"Laughing Willie added " Howlees fool wit
the wrong Hawaiians!

The two Hawaiian men helped the one sailor drag his buddies out the front door and too the street.

"Hey Bra... Don't come back." Willie had a big smile

Tony looked at the two women and chuckled. " I now know better than to mess with you two" That was the first time Tony and Keke had ever interacted.

Keiba, in the Hawaiian language means "Sunrise". In the culture of the island, the sunrise was inspiring and full of hope. Keke and her brothers last name was Aolani. Its meaning was used to remind people of the sky and its beautiful clouds. Keke defiantly embodied the spirit of her people. The Hawaiian sunrise and late night sky can make a person speechless with there beauty. Keke was that beautiful. Tony had never seen someone that looked like her. As she walked from place to place with such a fluid grace, Tony could not look anywhere else. She had long black free flowing hair. Her very dark tanned skin covered the smooth surface of her face and the rest of her body. The black eyebrows almost connected and followed the sensuous curve of her eyes. Keke's nose was very sleek with small nostrils. And her lips were almost a violet color that surrounded perfectly white teeth and help form a unique smile.

Tony carefully approached Keke.

"Hello! My name is Anthony. I'm so sorry you had to deal with those three idiots."

"Well, thank you" she paused and looked over Anthony from head to toe. He was in his usual colorful shorts and his white shirt was unbuttoned, exposing his muscular tanned chest.

She smiled at him" It's nice to know that you can take care of yourself. I won't have to worry about protecting you"

She smiled again.

Keke began to join Kemo, Willie and Tony on the beach every morning for a warm swim and when the surf was right, paddle out and catch some waves. In the late evenings when they were not working, the four would make a fire and cook fish that they had caught during the day and drink Pog. Pog is a Hawaiian drink made of passion,orange and guava juices. Tony would add a dark rum or some vodka to give it a little kick! Willie, the youngest of the three Aolani family would play his ukulele and Keke would dance the hula as the sun would set. She had taken lessons from her mother, who had learned it from her mother. The hula would tell stories of the old days when King Kamehameha was the King. It would also tell stories of the great war between the tribes of Hawaii for control of the islands. She could also tell about when the first white people came to the islands. The way she moved her hands, tiny hips and well defined arms was a sight that Tony had never seen before either. The way in which Keke moved, along with her facial expressions added to her unique beauty.

Keke had never been off of the small island. She was very curious about what the world was like off of Maui. With the backdrop of the Island of Lani and the Auau Channel between the two islands, Tony would "talk story" to Keke. He told her all about the great city of San Francisco and its tall buildings and great harbor. He tried to explain the Golden Gate Bridge but Tony wasn't that good with descriptive words. They would walk hand in hand along the beach. The evenings were always warm, not hot because of the breeze from the ocean. This was way different from the time he spent on the beaches of Okinawa and Guadalcanal. These beaches of Hawaii were quiet and calm. They almost never saw anyone else. It was like their own private place. No bloody bodies, no machine guns and mortars, and no zig zag running to avoid bullets.

"Anthony. Please tell me what it was like on those other islands? Okinawa, and how do you say.. Guadalcanal?"

Tony would walk in silence and look straight ahead. He wanted to forget. He knew if he started to tell her anything, he would begin to break down. And he didn't want to do that.

"Keke, ... I can't. It's too ugly. I don't think I could put into words well enough what happened.. What I did and what I saw."

They continued to walk back towards the main road where they had placed their bikes in some bushes. As Keke looked over at Tony, she could see the pain in his face and a tear rolling off of his check.

They road the bikes back to Keke's little cottage off of Front Street in silence. She occupied the second floor room which over looked the Lahina Harbor. They had to walk up an outside stair case to get to the door of the room. In her small room, was a bed, a night stand with a lamp, a dresser and a wash basin with a pitcher of water and a towel. There was no window. Just an opening, with dark colored drapes that were tied back to give the room a great view of the harbor. The wall as covered by wood from coconut trees, giving the room a dark color. Keke also had a small ice box that kept some fruit and a bottle of champagne cold.

Keke went to the ice box and took out the champagne, and a bowl of cut golden melons and several pieces of square chocolate.

This beautiful young Hawaiian woman looked at Tony. She raised her right hand over her mouth with her four finger raised as if to say "shush".

Standing as tall as she could, Keke began to unbutton Tony's flowered shirt. After the fourth button was undone, the shirt opened up showing off his muscular chest and tanned skin. She reached inside the shirt with both hands along his chest to help the shirt fall slowly to the floor.

Tony looked down at Keke and slowly began to unbutton the four buttons of the same blue colored flowered blouse she was wearing. He placed his hands inside the blouse to her shoulders to help it fall to the floor. She was still in her white swim suit. The bright white suit really helped make her tanned defined arms and shoulders stand out.

Keke then stepped very close to Tony and slowly, with a hand on each of his hips, slid his swim suit to the floor. His tanned upper body ended with a white line around his waste and then resumed at mid thigh. Tony's fully exposed body stood in the breeze that was coming in from the opening in the wall. The breeze was very warm and felt good to the both of them.

Tony then reached out to the shoulders of this enchanting dark woman and slowly and genitally pulled the straps of her suit down along her sides to her waste and finally to the floor. Even with her already brownish skin, Tony could still see the lines of her tanned natural color, giving her an erotic look to her naked body.

As the two naked bodies stood facing each other, the multi colored sky outside the opening, silhouetted them as it set. There bodies started to sweat from the heat of the late afternoon and from the moment.

Without a word being said up to this point, they would continue to communicate by touch and the energy each other was giving off. Looking up into Tony's eyes, Keke began to explore Tony's body. She worked both of her hands around his neck and shoulders. Using different pressures with her long fingers and swaying her hips, it felt as if she was telling a story using hula movements. Keke would work her hands in big and small circles in a massage type technique. While working down Tony's heaving chest with her hands, she kissed both of his nipples and placed her teeth around them causing a sensation close to pain but a feeling of pleasure. With her long black hair parted down the middle of her head, Tony began to intertwine his fingers in it as he lightly massaged her head. After circling Tony's nipples with her tongue, she moved her hands over his chest muscles and caressed them. Her fingers then followed the two long scares just below his arm pits that crossed his ribs. She then moved her hands lower to his eight packed stomach. She followed the contour of his muscles with the fingers of both hands. Tony continued to work his hands from her head to her shoulders as she lowered to one knee. The only sounds in the room came from the breeze and the couples heavy breathing.

Using her tongue and lips, Keke maneuvered her mouth around Tony's stomach and belly button while very lightly running her hands across his flexing hips.. They then moved around the large muscles under the dark hair of his rear end. She looked up to Tony with a sensual smile.

Tony placed his hands under her arms and lifted her up. Once on her feet feet, he placed his strong hands under the curved part of her rear end and raised her up. She wrapped her legs around his waste and her arms around his neck and shoulders to hold her in place. They found each others mouths and with continuing passion and electricity, they used their tongues to probe each others mouth. They closed their eyes and enjoyed the moments, not thinking of anything else but this beautiful feeling of excitement.

After this long and passionate embrace, Keke unfolded her legs and arms and stood in front of Tony. With a rather large smile on his face, Tony and Keke reversed roles. Tony worked his way down the front of Keke's long hairless body. Her brown skin glistened as she continued to sweat. Tony took his time exploring every inch of her body from her neck to her hips and butt checks. She would use her hands to guide his to places she wanted touched. He also used his tongue, teeth and lips to return the pleasures she gave to him. The time had seemed to stand still. But time was not an issue. Pleasing each other became the objective of this encounter. After several minutes of intense changing levels of pleasure, they removed their exhausted sweaty bodies to the cool soft open sheets of the awaiting bed.. They wrapped their arms and legs around each others wet bodies. With only now the sound of each others heavy tired breathing and the soft touch of each other, they prepared themselves for what they both knew what was coming next.

The next several weeks Keke and Tony spent many evenings together drinking champagne and dipping the cold melons into the melted chocolate before and after their sexual encounters. What disturbed Tony about all of this was that when he closed his eyes, he pictured Essa. He enjoyed his time with Keke. She was an awesome young woman. They had fun together , but Tony knew he wasn't in love with her. Something was missing between the two. Kemo knew what was going on between Keke and Tony. He liked Tony,but he wasn't Hawaiian.

"Hey bra. I like talk wit you 'bout Keke eh?"

"Sure Kemo. Whats up?"

"Ya know bra, you like a good friend. So, I need to talk honest wit you. You not Hawaiian. You and Keke look good now, but it never works out. Howlee and Hawaiian. She needs to be wit her own kind bra. If you make baby, what is it? White ?..... or Hawaiian? Tough on kid growing up. Where do you live? Keke would not be happy any where but Maui."

"Keke talk with you about this?"

"No. Just seen it before. Trust me."

"I'll give it some thought"

"Faster you end it, better for both of you." Kemo knew he was right about this

Tony spent a day or two thinking things over about his conversation with Kemo. Tony didn't have to think too hard.

He actually felt the same as Kemo, but he guessed he needed to be told. He spent the next two weeks seeing less and less of Keke. That was difficult because she was so beautiful and nice to him. He could tell that she knew something was up but was afraid to ask. Tony knew what he had to do,so he began to make plans for his exit. He had spent twenty two wonderful peaceful months on the island and he enjoyed all of them. He knew that he had to get back to life and that the Hawaiian life style wasn't what he wanted out of life. There was something better out there and he had to find it.

Tony used the phone in the Hotel to call his father and let him know that he was coming home. He wanted to go to school and use his GI Bill to pay for it. Dad was very excited. First to hear from Tony and second that he was coming home to go to school.

The conversation with Keke was difficult on both. She was in love him, but she also knew what Kemo had told Tony was true. Kemo actually had the same talk with Keke. They spent their final night together on their favorite beach, watching the sunset and the following morning the sun rise over the mountains to the east.

Tony found his way to Honolulu where he bought a ticket to fly home. He really didn't want to sail back. He'd done that adventure once, not again. Tony boarded the plane without any luggage or belongings. He was leaving the 85 degree December temperatures in Hawaii for who knows what in The City. The plane took off in the early afternoon and its path took them over Maui. He looked down on the little island paradise and smiled. It was exactly what he needed at the right time of his life. He would never forget

Keke and his friends Kemo and Willie. But Tony felt some excitement about his future and what it would bring.

CHAPTER NINE

The fight to San Francisco took six hours. Tony didn't sleep much on the flight. He had to plan his future before he got back to the mainland. Was he going to go to school? Where was he going to go to school? What was he going to study? He had some time to get things in order, but first things first. New Years Eve at Coit Tower. Would she be there?

The time spent with family and friends around Christmas is always special. Tony drank a lot of beer and ate some great food. It took him some time to adjust to the different food and cold weather. He got a part time job working at DeNikes Restaurant and Tavern down on Third and Galvez. He made sure he got a hair cut and bought the right kind of cloths so that he could fit in. It also would take him some time and effort to change the way he talked.

The last day of December came as Tony prepared to head over to North Beach and Coit Tower. The last time he went, it was just before midnight. This time he would get there earlier and hopefully run into Essa. He had asked his friends about her but they hadn't seen her or heard anything about what she was up to.

The evening came and went without any sight of Essa. Tony sat on the two foot wall that surrounded the parking lot and overlooked the City. He really had never noticed how beautiful it was. It didn't always have the five o'clock rainbow that Maui had, but it was different than any place on earth. The way it was built right up to the water front on all sides gave it a confined feeling. The tall buildings of the financial district together with all of the hilly winding streets, green parks, and churches was definitely different from the small island he had spent two years on. Sitting on that wall, Tony decided that he wanted something different in his already experienced life. He wanted to go to school using his GI Bill for payment and then enter law school. He had never considered that before but it just came to him out of the blue. But where? He would have to research schools and places. He did know that staying in San Francisco would carry too many memories of Essa and he had to leave again.

Rich Scrivner, Tony's best friend who was shot and killed in Okinawa and who he went through boot camp and training with at Paris Island, was from Bend Oregon, which is in Central Oregon. He had told Tony a lot about the state of Oregon. Rich was going to go back there and go to college. He wanted to play baseball and become a teacher coach. He talked about the few small schools that he was interested in.

So, Tony began to look into those schools. Linfield College in McMinnville. Lewis and Clark in Portland, Pacific University in Forest Grove and Willamette University in Salem.

Tony spent time in the near by library looking in to each school. They all had great qualities and seemed to be what he was looking for in a school. Willamette University stood out to him. It had a law school. He applied to each school and waited to to see which school would accept him for enrollment. He received great news that he had been accepted at each school! Now, he needed to figure out the best place for him. Again, Willamette University seemed to be the best place. It was in the States Capital City, it was in the middle of the state, it was a small town with a large town feel and the train station was right across the street from the school. Each school would accept his G.I. Bill payments, so Willamette was it. They also had a football team. He wrote the coach and told him of his interest and background. He was excited to have the ex-Marine join the squad.

As the train pulled into Salem Oregon, Tony looked at his watch. Eight in the morning. He had left the station in Oakland at 7:00 the night before. The trip was very uneventful, as he slept most of the night. The last hour he had a chance to see parts of the Willamette Valley as he traveled through Eugene, Corvallis and Albany. The California Zephyr, a new version of steam locomotives, made stops in all of those towns to pick up and drop off travelers.

Anthony Rucker's first look at Salem was from the train station located on 12th Street. It was surrounded by a long line of canneries several miles to the south and The Thomas Kay Woolen Mill to the north. Across the old two lane 12th Street sat Willamette University. From the station, Anthony walked across the street with his duffel bag full of his personal belongings sitting on his right shoulder.

Once across the street, he made his way on to the campus. It was a nice old and pretty campus. The small town feel was definitely there. It was lined with tall fir trees along its edges on two sides. The south part of campus had the Mill Creek running along it. The creek was partially covered by the old wooden grand stands of the football field. Next to the field on the east side was the gymnasium. The grand stands of the football field looked all the way across the open field to Eaton Hall. Eaton Hall, the library and Walton Hall were to the right side or east side of campus. Walton was right across the short path between it and the gymnasium. The other side of Eaton Hall was the Music building and the science building was on the corner of State and Winter Streets. Lausanne Hall, the oldest dormitory, faced Winter Street along he west border of the school.

Walking up to Walton Hall, which housed several foreign language classrooms and the offices of several professors, Anthony stopped two young ladies who were walking along the gravel pathway that went through the campus.

" Good Mooring ladies. Would you be so kind to tell me or point out Eaton Hall?"

"The second building that has the tower on top." as she pointed. "That building is the library." added the other girl.

"I'm going to be a student hear this fall and I need to

find the business office. " Anthony said with an excited reply and a smile.

The girls didn't seem to impressed with his appearance. He was dressed in the clothes he slept in all night and he needed a shave. The bag on his right shoulder had USMC - RUCKER printed on it and it caught the eyes of the girls.

The blonde girl looked at him and said "see ya around Rucker." and smiled.

After taking care of his registration and paying some basic fees, Anthony was directed to Lausanne Hall on the west side of the campus. He was going to have the chance to stay in a single room in the old dormitory. Construction was taking place behind Lausanne for a new dormitory which would be for females only. Across the street from Lausanne was the Willamette University Law School.

The next four years at Willamette University, from June of 1949 to May of 1952 saw many changes and additions on the campus as well as off campus. Baxter Hall was built across campus close to Walton Hall. It was a large brick building with two wings attached to it. The main section housed both male and female students. The wings on the west and east sides became home to four fraternities. Two on each wing. On the south side border of campus, five beautiful very large colonial style homes with sleeping porches were built to house the five new sororities.

The old grand stands for the football field came down to make room for the new state of the art Smith Auditorium.

This would now house all of the music departments programs along with the speech and debate programs. The new football field, McCulloch Stadium, would be built in Salem's Bush Park. The stadium was walking distance from the south west side of campus across Mission Street and the hospital. The new modern facility built with steel and concrete, was home to a training room, a visitors looker room, home team locker room, coaches offices,lights for night games and a large press box. It also had a full eight lane 440 yard cinder track. Next to the game field was a large practice field and the Willamette University baseball field. The new stadium would be able to seat at least 5,000 people and would be used for many outside activities including graduation. With the football field gone, the middle of the campus had what would be called the Quad. It was an open grass field with walking paths that the students could use for various activities.

Anthony enjoyed all of the new and exciting campus. He played football on the varsity team for all four years. He found that he still loved playing the game. Anthony was older than almost all of the players and even a few of the coaches. His age gave him a physical and mental advantage. At the age of 28, Anthony was now 190 pounds and a full six foot two inches tall.

Anthony had a different outlook on practice and games from his teammates and opponents. He had been through the most difficult training as a Marine Raider. He had been through some of the most horrific situations war had to offer.. He had watched his friends dye. He had killed. Football now was just a game. He loved and had missed working with others for a common goal. He also knew how to lead and how and when to follow. Football was fun.

Finally, school for him had become important. In high school, he just went through the motions and did as little as possible. Now, he wanted to learn. His first year was learning how to learn and study. "Pops" as his teammates called him, didn't get involved in many of the things that the younger guys did. He didn't join in the fraternity programs and activities. He was already a part of the strongest brotherhood. He stayed away from the parties and dating college age girls. "Pops" had a goal of becoming a lawyer and he knew he had to have great grades and, pass the LSAT test. He would also have to have the ability to focus, to research and to get his points across through speech.

Anthony spent the first year living in the dorm, using his GI bill money to pay for school ect. He did find a part time job after football season working in the canneries along 12 Street and rented a small one bedroom apartment near campus. Salem was such a small town, and everything he needed was in walking distance, he didn't need a car. He did have a bike just in case he had to make a long trip across town. He also had to get used to all of the rain. The rains came in October, the snow in December and with the winds that blew off of the near by Willamette River it was a lot colder than The City had ever been.

Tony did get involved with the Army ROTC program. It was a two year course taught by major Norman Campion. It provided him a chance to learn how to speak in front of people,stay focused and research information on projects. By the end of his Senior year, Anthony was the highest ranking student and even began teaching some classes on self defense. Also his Senior year, Anthony met and began dating a local girl who was not a student at Willamette.

Anthony met Amara Espisito while he was working at one of the canneries on 12th Street. Amara was a 23 year old who had been working in the office of the building since she had graduated from Salem High School. She was a tall thin young lady with dark long hair past her shoulders. Some times she wore it up to give her a different look. She kind of reminded him of Janessa, but not as pretty. Not being a warehouse worker and being a secretary she always dressed in the latest styles and looked great every day. Since she was so attractive, all of the men, even the married ones, were constantly making passes at her. Anthony, on the other hand didn't. He was always nice and smiled, but very seldom engaged in conversation with her.

Anthony always went to Mass at St. Josephs Catholic Church on Saturday nights. With it being Easter, Anthony went to mass on this April 1951 Sunday morning. He was sitting towards the back near his normal place at the end of the pew. It was very crowded and Amara unknowingly sat right next to him. She didn't recognize him as he was well dressed and shaved. As they walked back from receiving communion, she was in front of him. Getting to the pew first, he had to move in front of her as he sat down. They looked at each other and realized whom they had been sitting next to. After the Mass they talked for a few minutes on the steps leading up to the church. They shared some laughs and small talk. From that point on, they both made an effort to talk when they could at work. Finally, Anthony decided that he should invite her out to see a movie.. The problem was neither had a car, So they waked. Anthony and Amara walked to the Elsinore Theater which was downtown on the other side of

Willamette University. They saw "The Greatest Show on Earth", which won the Academy Award for best picture. Betty Hutton, Cornell Wilde, James Stewart and Carlton Heston were the stars of the movie. The walk to and from the Elsinore on this beautiful late spring evening helped make the conversation between the two easy and very pleasant. Amara listened to Anthony talk about some of his past and what he wanted to do going forward. She would ask him questions that he easily answered. He found talking to her to be very easy. He was definitely very different and more interesting than anyone she had ever met or talked with before. She also thought that he was very handsome.

Amara lived with her parents in a small house east of the canneries on Standard Avenue just across the street from Aldrich Park. Tony lived real close to her. Two and a half blocks north on the corner of Ferry and 16th,, was Anthony's one bedroom apartment in the basement of an old home.

The next several months, Anthony and Amara spent time together in the park, eating picnic lunches, talking and sometimes just reading in the quiet. They both enjoyed this very different type of relationship. It was simple and stress free. Neither trying to impress each other, but enjoying a great friendship. They even borrowed Amara's parents car for a one day trip to the beach in Newport. Both knew that things would change when August and September came around . Anthony would be starting his final year of football and his Senior year of studies at Willamette.

Because of Anthony's busy schedule, Amara and Anthony only were able to see each other on weekends. Tony had saved enough money to buy himself a 1946 Plymouth

Coupe. It had two doors and was his favorite color ,blue. The engine was a six cylinder 217 cubic inch motor with 95 horse power. IT had no heater , but it did have a radio in it! Anthony loved his music and so did Amara. They would go to Sunday morning Mass at 10:30 together and then drive across the Willamette River bridge to West Salem. There was a small park on a hill that overlooked the river where they would sit on a blanket, eat a lunch and listen to the radio while right next to the car.

Johnnie Ray's "All of Me" and " A Summer Am I" were popular songs at the time. Johnnie just happened to be from near by Dallas Oregon. Tony Bennett's "Here Is My Heart" and "Stay Where You Are" along with Billie Holiday's "I Only Have eyes For You" and "Blue Moon" were some of their favorites. Their absolute favorite singer though was Frank Sinatra. His big hits were "If You Are But A Dream" and "Nancy".Amara,s favorite was "Put Your Dreams Away".

Anthony's last season of football began with a new Head Coach. Ted Ogdahl. He had just completed a stint of high school coaching, where he had won three of the last four state championships at Grant High School in Portland. Coach Ogdahl had played for the famous Amos Stagg at Pacific University. Things were very different under his leadership. Anthony could tell this new coach was going to be very good. The coach moved "Pops" from playing on the interior defensive line to what coach called End. In this position, Pops no longer started in a four point stance but on his feet. This allowed him to see things better, use his speed and athletic ability to make plays.. He loved it. The Bearcats didn't win the league championship but they were close. They won five games,lost two and tied two. Anthony was rewarded for his good play by being named to the all conference second team on defense.

Anthony made many friendships with the players on the team. He found himself drawn to the many players that came from the Hawaiian Islands. He was taken in by them early on probably, because he understood them better than the mainland guys. He could also talk with them in the local Hawaiian slang. He never really let them know of his time on Maui. This was a close nit group of young men. A few of the Hawaiian guys had served in the war and were using their G.I. Bill to pay for school. Most were there because Willamette wanted to have a more diverse population of students. These kids served two purposes, they were classified as a different race and they were involved in extracurricular athletics. A few of them came from the inter city schools on Honolulu but the majority had attended the prestigious private schools. Kamehameha, Iolani, Damian and Punahou High Schools provided most of the students. The public school students that played football were a tough breed. Very physical and hard nosed. They took some time to trust the white players. The white culture of Salem Oregon in the 1940's was difficult to get used to. Even though the students didn't spent a lot of time in the community, the culture on campus was much the same. Even Tony had trouble fitting in. Growing up in San Francisco, which is a large city, is not the same as the small town of Salem. Many of the Hawaiian athletes and students became homesick and left at the Christmas break and didn't come back.

The one main lander that Tony really got along with was Pete Dickson. Pete was from Scoby Montana. Everyone just called him "Scoby". Scoby was a skinny offensive lineman as a freshman. He spent all of his extra time lifting weights with the Hawaiian kids trying to get heavier. He also ate five meals a day. He would spend his summers back in Montana working on the family farm. By the time he was a Senior, Pete was the biggest and strongest player on the team. He was also very smart. He always brought home A's for grades. His classes were always the highest level Math classes along with Biology and Chemistry. Scoby was also noted for his often times ragging temper. For some reason, Tony could calm him down and keep him from hurting other students. In the evenings, when Pete was studying, no one made any noise near his dorm room. Pete did like to drink his beer. Especially after games. Before Tony met Amara, Pete and Tony would drink plenty of beer after games in Pete's dorm room. Tony needed to dull the head aches he would have from the contact and Pete used the beer to calm himself. After an hour or so, Tony would leave and Scoby would study the rest of the night. After graduating from Willamette, Pete would enter Medical school at the University of Washington. He always wanted to be a small town doctor somewhere.

Anthony also noticed that the girls of Willamette really were not there for an education. Many of the girls came from rich families. Their parents were doctors, lawyers and business people. They took classes but seemed more interested in the social activities of the school. He felt that they were looking for their future husband. Anthony made sure he stayed away from those type of young ladies. Plus they were so young. Most 18 and 19 year old girls were not interested in a poor and old guy who played football and drove a beat up old car everywhere.

Amara would attend all of Anthony's home games

and any of the close ones. She had learned how to drive Anthony's old Plymouth, so that she could make many of his games. After the away games that Amara made, Anthony would drive the both of them back to Salem. On the way back Anthony would answer questions about the game and football itself. Amara was trying to understand the game. They always went to dinner on Saturday nights at a restaurant in West Salem, which was across the Willamette River. It was called The Eola Inn. It had seating that overlooked the the river. It also had a Piano Bar and a 50 room hotel. After dinner they would enjoy the music and each other by dancing to the different tunes. After Tony's last game, which was in McMinnville Oregon against arch rival Linfield College, they again stopped at The Eola Inn for dinner and dancing. It began to slowly snow, which was unusual for this time of the year. It was a beautiful sight watching the snow falling on the river below them as well as in the distance. Anthony enjoyed a nice dinner of fresh in shell crab with mashed potatoes gravy along with an artichoke dipped in olive oil and red vinegar. Amara went with some also fresh salmon with rice and broccoli with a white gravy. They shared a bottle of a Merlot.

"Anthony! With seafood ,we are supposed to drink a white wine!" Anthony laughed and replied

"So much for following the rules. My father always said to drink what you enjoy. And we both like Merlot!"

He held up his half full wine glass towards Amara. As they toasted he said "Hear is to the both of us".

After dancing and for Anthony, several Manhattans, and for Amara two Shaken Martini's, Anthony asked Mitch for the bill.

"Hey Tony, your not thinking about crossing the bridge tonight are you?"

"Sure thing Mitch."

Mitch was always their waiter. He was an interesting guy. He too served in the Marine Corp during the war and was also on Okinawa. Just like Tony, he was using his G.I. Bill to pay for school at Willamette. Instead of playing football , he played baseball. The Dumpster, as he called himself, was one of the funniest people Tony had ever met. He gave everyone a nickname and was responsible for Tony being called Pop's. And could he tell a story! When Tony was not out with Amara, he and Mitch would get together. They both saw the same shit during the war and could talk about it. Unless you were there, it was difficult to understand what they felt. They became very close friends and later in life they would continue to stay in touch. Mitch was a lot like Rich!

"Well not tonight Tony. They closed the bridge going over the river for the night. Way too much ice". Mitch shrugged his shoulders.

"If you want, I can hook you up with a room that has a nice view of the river?"

Amara quickly answered the Dumpster " That would be really nice of you Mitch. We'll wait hear until you set things up."

Tony was a bit suppressed at her quick answer. In the

1950's it wasn't a practice to rent rooms to couples who were not married, but Dumpster took care of things. Anthony left a big tip after another round of drinks.

As they sipped that last drink "Ah. What about your parents? They will worry"

"No problem. I'll just call and explain the situation. They will understand. It's pretty dangerous crossing that river on that old bridge." She winked.

Anthony bought a bottle of Merlot from the bar and as they walked by a candy machine, Anthony also bought a chocolate candy bar.

"Whats that for?" Amara asked

"The wine brings out the pure taste of the chocolate" He winked and they walked to the room holding hands.

"Check this out!" Anthony opened the drapes on the window. The room overlooked the river looking south. It was a different view than that they always had at the restaurant. This looked the length of the Willamette River as it flowed south towards Albany.

"Oh Anthony. That's beautiful. Dumper was right about the view. " It was really snowing hard now.

"Let's sit and watch and listen" She opened the window , turned off the light in the room and grabbed a blanket off of the bed. They moved the small couch away from the wall and put it in front of the window.

"Its so quiet" Amara cuddled up against Anthony

"Yep And its cold too"

They had talked about many things in the past and making love was one of them. Anthony knew how difficult it was to get involved with someone on that level and then having to end the relationship. He didn't want to go through that again. Anthony had not told Amara about that part of his time in Hawaii.

Amara had had a boy friend in high school, but never reached the point of experiencing love making. Amara wanted to be sure that her first experience would be with someone she really loved and that someone really loved her.

Anthony thought the world of Amara. She was smart, very pretty and enjoyed the same things he did. He had thought about the possibility of marriage to her. Several things though kept him from talking about marriage with her. First, he knew he wanted to become a lawyer, but he didn't have the money to continue on with law school. He had visited with his old First Lieutenant from Okinawa, who was now Captain Michael Erb. He was visiting colleges ROTC programs around the country and stopped in at Willamette. He suggested to Anthony to rejoin the Marine Corp by enrolling into the Officers Candidate School. It would be a lifetime commitment but he would be able to go through law school with the Marines and become a JAG lawyer. Anthony didn't think Amara would want to be moving around a lot as the wife of a Marine Officer. Plus, he would be gone for long periods of time while attending school.

Second. He wasn't sure how much he loved her. He knew there are several levels of love. Trying to figure out what level they were at was still a question. Third, he still could not get Janessa out of his mind. He didn't know what she was doing at this time.

Mike, his old friend from the neighborhood, had run into Janessa at The St. Francis Hotels bar. She was on a date with, who else, Bradley. They were not married and they were not together either. Janessa had asked Mike about Tony. Mike had told her that the two of them wrote letters to each other and occasionally talked on the phone. Mike gave her an update on Tony's life in Salem while he was attending Willamette. He included Tony playing football and that he was dating someone very special. Tony was also considering re joining the Marines. Essa thanked Mike for the info and told Mike to say hello to Tony for her and gave Mike her phone number to give to Tony. Mike decided not to tell Tony about his conversation with Essa and not pass on the phone number.

There was just enough light shining through the window from outside so that they could see each other just fine. They held each other getting warm and watching the snow coming straight down.

After a bit, Amara then turned towards Anthony face and smiled. She gently kissed Anthony. Anthony returned her sweet kiss with a more passionate kiss. Not sure if it was the alcohol, the atmosphere or a combination of both, but Amara opened her mouth and moved her tongue to probe his mouth. It had been such a long time since Anthony experienced such a feeling and he returned the same type of kiss meeting her tongue with his. The wool blanket had kept them very warm, so when it fell to the floor they stopped the kiss. Amara stood up, closed the window and began to unbutton her blouse with a seductive smile on her face . The light from outside was perfectly placed on her face. It really brought out and enhanced the shape of her eyes. They weren't round, but the shape fit her face and with her brown eyes and very long lashes, Anthony was almost mesmerized. He thought to himself, how beautiful her face was. When she turned, it exposed a somewhat long and tight skinned neck that glistened.

"Are you sure about this? Anthony questioned her.

Without a word, she pulled back her hair and leaned over him exposing her open blouse, black lace bra and full breasts. While her hair fell in front of her face , she then began to unbutton Anthony's shirt. Soon they were both standing and naked to the waist. Amara had seen Anthony with his shirt off before at the beach. She had never touched him there tough.. She began to move her hands over his warm but moist chest and through the small amount of hair. Amara followed her fingers over his two knife scars on his side and the area on his arm wear he was hit by the bullet in Okinawa. After softly kissing his neck , she worked her way to his right nipple and circled it several times with her tongue. Using her teeth, she gently bit it. She moved to his left side doing the same thing while her hands worked their way to his hips and lower body. Anthony worked his hands through her hair and then to her neck to massage her shoulders. With both on their knees facing each other, Anthony moved his hands to her breasts as their mouths met and opened up. Her skin was so soft, but firm and had a very nice aroma to it. She to was moist from the heat of the blanket and also from the pleasure of skin against skin. As Anthony softly and gently massage Amara's chest as he placed his thumb and forefingers around her erect nipples. She pulled her head away from him, looked up and tilted her head back,with a slight moan and smile. She then grabbed Anthony's hair with both hands and enjoyed the moment.

Anthony had only been with Amara at the beach in Newport a couple of times. She had always worn a bathing suit that covered most of her upper body. So, seeing her in just the little amount of light without anything on above her waist was really exciting to Anthony.

He knew from his time with Keke, that taking his time and being gentle was going to be very important when it came to pleasing Amara. He wanted her to enjoy this moment. Amara's body was shaped as well as he had hoped and thought it was. The feel of her skin to his hands and body was soft and very warm. Instead of exploring her the way she did with him, Anthony em-breast her. Pressing his chest against hers and moving his hands up and down her back. He also gently touched her above her hips as they open mouthed kissed.

Anthony undid the back of her skirt. As it fell to the floor, he slowly pulled her white underpants to the carpeted floor as she stepped out of them. Anthony could only marvel at what she was looking at. Amara had a very slim but muscular body. Her hips were small and her skin was tight. She also had a small belly button. Her backside was very curvy and firm. He could almost hold her checks in his large hands. Soon they were under the blanket again both naked.

Anthony new, because of his time with Keke, several ways to pleasure a woman. With this being Amara's first time they spent an hour exploring each other under the blanket. Needing more room, they moved to the bed. Once in a more comfortable place and easier to move around, Anthony didn't have to worry about cramping up. He usually did after games. Anthony knew that if he could get Amara to relax a little more, she would enjoy things much more. Taking his time he kissed around her pelvic area. He would insert his tongue into her to stimulate and arouse her. He would also slip his fingers to the same spot to give her different sensations. He knew when he was in the right place when she began to squirm and make slight moaning noises. She reached a climax several times and became very wet and relaxed. She got to a point where she really wanted Anthony all of the way inside of her. Anthony positioned himself so that he could be inside of her and also place his hands in other places. After they both came to climax at the same time, they laid on their sides and faced each other , very exhausted! Anthony was afraid to fall asleep. He didn't want to frighten her with the sounds he made while dreaming of his experiences in the war. He often woke up yelling orders. He often would see the face of his first kill. All of that would ruin this already wonderful evening. Amara would eventually wake up and start to kiss Anthony and arouse him. They would explore a little more but get to a different position with her sitting on her knees on top of Anthony with him inside of her. She could then control the rhythm while Anthony again used both of his hands on her breasts.

Anthony placed the covers over Amara to keep her warm while he went into the bathroom. He started the shower to get the water to a warm almost hot temperature. Just as he was stepping in the shower, Amara walked in just behind him. After rinsing them selves, Anthony took the soap and began to wash Amara. With the water off. It was still warm from the steam of the water. He covered her with the lather and massaged it into her skin.

"Two can play this game."

Amara took the soap and lathered things up on Anthony. She then put her hands around his neck and hopped a little and placed her legs around Anthony's hips. Things were a little slippery but they made love right there. While she was still around Anthony and he inside of her, she turned the shower on. The water came out warm and quickly heated up, which added to the sensation.

"That was a nice touch" Anthony smiled.

While eating breakfast at the hotel restaurant, Amara explained to Anthony that there was no way of her getting pregnant because of the timing of her cycle. Birth control at that time did not come with a pill. Many relied on knowing their minstrel cycle. Two days later she let Anthony know that she started her period.

The next few weeks, the couples relationship grew stronger. Amara always had a smile and their conversations began to become more serious. One question that see had was about Anthony's tattoo on his upper back. It was two capitol letters, R and S over R.I.P.

" Anthony what does that mean" When she question

him.

R is for Rich, the S is for Scrivner. RIP is Rest In Peace. Rich and I meet the first day of Boot Camp. We were the best of friends all the way through. We both decided to do the Raider training together. On our first leave, we had the Initials put on each others back. I had his back going forward and he had mine. I guess I didn't to a very good job of having his. I lost him at Oky. When I got back to the States, I added R. I. P. I think of him often. Anthony just stared off looking at nothing.

They also talked a lot about what Anthony was going to do and about how she would fit in.

Christmas vacation rolled around. Anthony was planning a trip to the City as he always did, but this time he wanted to bring Amara along with him. They took the train because it would be faster and safer. He wasn't sure the old Plymouth would make it down and back. Plus, there was always the possibility of snow and ice on the roads.

"We could always spend the night in a hotel somewhere if we get caught in the snow again!" Amara grabbed Anthony around the waist and gave him a hug and a big smile.

Anthony's parents met them in Oakland. They stayed at his parents home, but in separate rooms. Anthony got use of his old Ford that he left there years ago. Dad kept it around for the boys to use when they were still living there.

Tony, as he was known at home, showed Amara around the City. She had read about San Francisco and looked at pictures of it I magazines, but they didn't do it justice. They also spent an afternoon and evening down the peninsula in the little town of San Bruno. Mike lived there with his wife Edith. Some of the old gang of friends, Sean Hannon and Jim Ross, came over and they enjoyed dinner and many Martini's. Mike as well as Sean, both enjoyed shaking and drinking them. He also had a very nice and sometimes lowed music system. Many of the favorite artists were listened too, especially Frank Sinatra! Amara fit right in with Sinatra and the Martinis.

Tony was in the kitchen with Mike getting an other round of drinks when Mike looked at Tony

"Ruck! You son of a bitch. You did it again. You hit another Jack Pot with Amara."

"Thanks my friend. She is special."

"When is the Date?"

"What date?"

"You dumb ass, when are you getting married?"

"Oh. Haven't got that far yet."

"Well, you better hurry, cause she might figure out that she could do a lot better!!"

Tony held up his middle finger on is left hand. " Keep shaking my friend."

It was obvious to everyone there that Tony and Amara

had something special. And Amara defiantly got the approval of all that were there.

When school started up again in January, Anthony and Amara returned to the grind of work and school. Anthony, after much thought, went to the Marine recruiting office in downtown Salem. He had spent time there before talking to Gunnery Sargent Parker about his possibilities if he signed up. On this trip, he made the commitment to enroll in the Officers Candidate School as soon as he graduated from Willamette University. The war in Korea had been going on, and the Marines wanted soldiers. Anthony signed with the written agreement that his MOS would be attending law school if he passed the Law SAT. This was his way to become a lawyer without having to pay any money.

Amara wasn't real happy with Anthony's decision. She knew all along that he wanted to become a lawyer, but she thought that he would find away to do it at Willamette's Law School.

They spent as much time together as possible

and making love when it was possible. It was still a time that they both enjoyed and looked forward too. Each time they would experiment with new and different ways to please each other. When it came to making love, they both got eminence pleasure out of it. Amara couldn't conceive of someone who could make her feel as good as Anthony did. Anthony also enjoyed his time with Amara, but just like Keke, something was missing. He didn't know what it was, but he just knew.

Anthony graduated on Mothers Day in May 1953 and

was in Quantico Virginia six days later. OCS, Officers Candidate School, would last four months. This training would be difficult. Getting men ready for war was hard but getting Officers, who had never been a Marine ready, was not an easy task. Every Marine no matter what their job (MOS) was, they has to be a rifleman first. After passing OCS, the next step of five months would also be spent at Quantico at what was called The Basic School (TBS). This school would train them in leadership skills, decision making, war strategy ,navigation, communication and many other skills. While at both schools, Anthony would not be allowed to call or receive any phone calls. He was allowed to write one letter per week. He usually only had enough time to write only one letter. He was only allowed mail after the first month of OCS. So for the first month, Anthony could not communicate with Amara or his parents. Anthony and his parents had gone through this before when he enlisted, but Amara had not.

The first few months, Amara would write almost every other day to Anthony. She would receive a letter from him about once every two weeks until TBS started in October. The letters from each began to really slow down. Amara was lonely for Anthony and missed him so much. So few letters from Anthony was a little disheartening. Unfortunately she began to get used to not having him around and got back into her old life. Anthony missed Amara also, but he was so busy it became easier for him to not think of her. Just before he graduated from TBS in February, he was told that he passed his LSAT and that his Military Occupational Specialty (MOS) would be in Newport Rhode Island for an additional two years. This would be his beginning of law school.

Need less to say, this put a large strain on the relationship of Anthony ans Amara. Even though the war was over in Korea, Anthony had no idea of where his duty station would be after completing his MOS.

The two continue to write each other their feelings about the situation. They finally talked it over on a long expensive phone call. With tears in both of their eyes and shaking voices, they both agreed to end the relationship. Both hoping for the best for each other. Anthony would continue to send Amara a card on Valentines Day, until it came back as no longer living at this address in 1956. Amara had moved on in her life. She married the son of the man that owed the cannery in which she worked.

Anthony's time in Rhode Island was very difficult. He was a slow reader and was not fast at typing, all skills the other Marines possessed. Fortunately for Anthony, his retention was very good. The time spent at Willamette taught him how to learn. With his free time, which was very little, he continued with his training in the field of self defense. Because of his past qualifications and combat experiences, Anthony was able to obtain his Martial Arts Instructors Trainer (MAIT) certification. During his time as an enlisted Marine, he had obtained the highest level of Black Belt. He enjoyed training others and often sparred with other Marine trainers.

Tony, as he was now called by his fellow Marine attorneys, flew home for Christmas as he had a two week leave. Again he spent time with his parents and family. Brothers Paul and Robert had both finished college and were working in the area. Paul was married and teaching at a Junior High school in San Bruno and Bob had moved with his wife to San Jose to start his career as a police officer. Joyce was still living at home and working at the near by phone company.

The vacation would also bring together the old friends at the usual place. Mike's house in San Bruno.. Jim Ross and Sean Hannon brought along their wives, leaving their children with a family baby sitter. Rob Silver also showed up! He was living in Seattle working for an oil company doing a lot of work buying up property in Alaska. He thought that they wanted to drill more oil in the supposedly rich fields and then build an oil pipeline to the states.

Mike as always, enjoyed Bar-B-Q ing for everyone. Always music and plenty of Martinis. Of course Tony and Rob talked about their activities of the past. They both had been gone much of the time after they all graduated from high school. Tony made it clear that he would not talk about his time during the war. And he did have to hear about Amara.

"Tony my man. Your a dumb shit!. How could you let Amara get away? Or did she finally come to her senses?"

Mike was always straight to the point about every thing.

"She was perfect for you."

Tony would just smile and shrug his shoulders. Explaining the situation was too difficult and it kind of hurt to talk about it. He was still hiding what he felt. He did learn in the Marines that "It is what it is. Deal with it."

On that New Years Eve of 1959, Tony arrived at the Saint Francis Hotel at 1700. Jim, Sean, Rob and 'little Willy",

Chris Wilhelm all walked through the front doors with their wives together. Mike was early of course.

They all sat at a large table. Mike had called in favor from the Head Waiter to get such great accommodations. The dinner was served and all enjoyed their meals. They then went into the lounge where there would more drinks, some dancing and the New Years celebration. Little Willy was at the main bar ordering some drinks when a rather large ugly guy pushed Willy knocking the drinks to the floor.

"Get out of my way" Said the oaf while looking down at Chris

"Excuse me Sir, but you should pay for those spilled drinks."

"Kiss my ass. Your lucky I don't hurt you."

Tony saw the whole situation unfolding and was right there.

"Well partner! You need to rethink those words." Tony was about two inches shorter and about 30 pounds lighter. He was wearing a long sleeve coat that was very loose fitting. The sleeves covered his rather large biceps, forearms and chest. Running everyday, lifting weights three times a week and sparring on the other days had kept Tony in fighting shape. Always a Marine!

"This ain't any of your business flat top. Shove off." Flat top, Tony figured it referred to his high and tight marine hair cut.

Tony smiled and replied" I just made it my business partner. " There was a pause as they looked into each others eyes.

Tony continued " You have two choices, Pay for the drinks or pay for the drinks and leave! Which is it going to be?"

"Neither. How about you and me outside flat top. Like right now."

Tony smiled again " That's not one of the choices partner. And might I add not a good one! But.. OK. Lets go get busy."

Holding up his hand to Chis to stay " I'll be right back. Meet you at the table."

Tony walked calmly in front of the big oaf towards the door and the street.. Suddenly he had his coat pulled over his head. Rookie mistake Tony thought. With his hands over his head and punches being landed to his sides, he quickly wriggled out of his coat and freed himself. Now he was real mad. The oaf was surprised at how fast Tony was. Tony's first punch landed right on target. The nose. Blood immediately began to pour as the guy stumbled backwards. Tony followed up with his left hand right to the throat of the guy and he squeezed with just enough pressure to force the man to his knees. Two quick punches to the jaw finished this confrontation before any body saw it.

The Doorman came in from the outside and saw the oaf crumpled up on the floor and looked at Tony.

"You OK Pal? Let me help you pay for those drinks. " Tony looked at the Doorman

"He's had too much to drink and owes the bar for his last round."

Tony reached into the guys back pocket and grabbed his wallet. He took out a twenty and tossed the wallet back on top of him.

"You might want to call a cab for him." Tony started back to the bar.

Tony picked up his coat from the floor and walked back into the bar area. He handed Chris the twenty.

"Our friend changed his mind. He said to keep the change."

The party continued and all were having a great time. At 2200, Tony excused himself from the party. He briefly explained that certain types of load noises, such as bangs and fire crackers, fireworks brought back bad memories. His friends kind of understood. On his way out and to his car, there was a janitor cleaning up the blood stain on the carpet that the oaf had left.

By 10:30, Tony was at the top of Coit Tower. He held a bottle of white wine and two glasses in his coat pocket. Just in case. Several couples walked through the balcony over looking the City and its lights. It was cold but clear. Tony left a few minutes after midnight. He smiled, still remembering

Essa and their time together twenty years ago.

First Lieutenant Anthony Rucker returned to Newport a week later.

CHAPTER TEN

After Janessa talked with Mike at the Saint Francis Hotel, she began to think a lot more about Tony. Essa decided to end things once and for all with Brad. Mike had told her about Tony's relationship with Amara and his plans about making the Marine Corp a career. Tony was a really focused guy these days.

Janessa decided that she too needed to get going with her life. She had several jobs that really didn't have a future going forward. So, she enrolled at San Francisco State University and began taking graduate courses in business. She was going to put all of her energy and focus into starting a career in the business world. If Tony could focus and find a career, she would also.

Janessa completed her degree by December of 1954. She had several interviews with companies but being a woman in a mans world would be difficult. During an interview with Macy's, a very large high end department store with locations up and down the west coast, the Vice President noticed that her last name was Greek. He was also. He found Janessa a very smart and very pretty young lady. Some how her toughness came out in the interview and the Vice President was very impressed. Janessa received an offer to head up the cosmetic department of the San Francisco store. If she could turn around the non profit making department into one that made money, she would have chance at becoming the west coast cosmetic manager.

Janessa began to work hard at her new opportunity. The pay was good, but being elevated to the next level of management would really help pay her bills. She spent more time at 1700 O' Farrell Street than any other employee of Macy's. The cosmetic department , under her leadership, saw many changes. The way it was set up was the first change. The women who worked the department also made changes. They were required to dress differently and were told to use the products sold there. They were also required to keep up with the product information as well as learning new sales techniques. All of these changes showed in increased sales and prophets. Janessa performances were noted and appreciated.. After one year, she was promoted to the west coast manager position. Janessa would travel to the stores in Seattle, Portland, Los Angeles and San Diego. The changes she made in the San Francisco store were made at all of the other stores. Other departments in all of the stores started to use Janessa's new approach to sales to also increase sales. Janessa was soon promoted again to a Vice President position that dealt with improvements. Janessa was liked by all of the employees of the stores, but she was the only female in upper management. Being competitive, focused and tough, Janessa often intimidated her male peers. No one else carried themselves with as much confidence and beauty as she did.

After visiting Coit Tower on News Years of 1956, Essa found herself on the lonely side of life. She enjoyed her job, but at 35 years old and never having been married, she thought about having children. Through her job, Janessa met many very nice men. The men that were her age that were interesting were always married. Janessa finally met a nice man who was two years younger than her. He had just moved to the City from New jersey to work for The Bank of America on California Street.

Richard Tucker was a graduate of NYU's graduate school of Business. He needed a change in his life, so he came west to San Francisco. Like Janessa, he was a successful and hard worker. He to didn't have much time to meet many interesting people, let alone an interesting woman. So when he met Janessa, he became very enchanted with her. Buy the end of the year in December they became engaged. Janessa visited Coit Tower on New Years Eve of 1957 by herself just to be able to move on from Anthony.

Ten months later, Janessa and Richard brought a baby boy into the world. By July of 1959, baby number two, a little girl graced the couple

Janessa continued to work for Macy's making trips up and down the coast. Richard also continued to work at the Bank. Janessa's parents were more than happy to take care of the children whenever needed. The Tucker family had bought a modest home out in the Sunset District of The City, close to the beach. It was easy to get to work for both and it was planned to be a starter home for them with the idea of eventually moving South down the peninsula some where.

Having two children for any couple could complicate a marriage. And Janessa and Richards also became complicated. Transporting the children to day care, which was spendy, and too Janessa's parents home forced the two parents to take turns with the transportation. They also had to adjust many things because of Janessa's travel and job. Often times things would come up where she would have to leave with short notice. There wasn't a lot of together time for the couple. Richard wasn't a real fan of Janessa's wit, and her comments and jokes began to really wear on him. They began to argue over things that they had been able to work out in the past. Janessa contemplated cutting back at work. Maybe just continuing on at the San Francisco store was talked about, but the upper management wasn't very supportive. The two continued to struggle, hopeful that they could work their way through their issues. Thinking that when the children both reached school age, things would change. The idea of moving South, was put on hold. It would be impossible to have Janessa's parents watch the children.

Richard was moving up the ladder at the Bank of America. He was an expert at securing accounts of the many big businesses in The City. He was always gone in the evenings entertaining clients and would be clients. He was promoted to one of the Vice Presidents with the idea of becoming the President of Operations. The subject of divorce was talked about between the two. Divorce was something that was frowned upon buy most, especially big business. Both Janessa and Richard decided that it would be better for the family if Richard moved into and apartment close the family home. Maybe they would stop the arguing and repair their relationship. With that added expense, neither could cut back on work. Richard was again promoted to the President of Operations in December of 1962. With that came a very large pay increase . As they all settled into life with Richard spending less and less time around the children, They both decided to file for a divorce and it became final in July of 1963.

Once the divorce was final, Janessa's life didn't change much. She was happy in that she had two wonderful children to raise. If she ever became lonely, she just made sure she spent time with the kids. Francis her oldest, was a rambunctious little boy. He was tall for his age and very smart. He to had dark hair but it was curly, just like his fathers. His eyes were blue, also just like Richards. He was definitely

Richard's son. Francis, as his mother would call him, was an athletic young boy and very interested in always playing outside. He loved running around the near by park and playing on all of the equipment. Richard enjoyed taking Frank there whenever he had a chance. Richard too, had an athletic build but had never participated in any sports as a kid growing up. His schooling was always very important to him and his parents. Little Katerina was the identical small version of her mother. Her light brown hair covered an angel's delicate little face. At times Katerina seemed as fragile as a butterfly's wing's. This remarkable and charming little girl, covered up a tough as nails personality. Katerina could turn on the charm like a light switch and just as easily turn into a rough and tumble Tom Boy. Janessa knew that Katy, as she was called, was going to be a handful growing up, but a strong adult woman who would go far in life. All she had to do was figure out where she wanted go.

Richards visits with the children on the weekends was very regular through the first year but soon slowed. In the beginning of 1963 Richard was recruited by a coalition of regional associations in New York to compete with Bank of America. He had been instrumental in the development of the "BankAmericard" and its progress in the late 1950's and early 60's. The enticement to head this new coalition was just to hard to pass up. This association became the "Interbank" which started Master Charge, which would eventually become Master Card.

CHAPTER ELEVEN

Living in Washington D.C. in the early sixties was perfect for Tony. He could really jump into his job as a Navy Jag attorney. He had almost no distractions. He lived in the basement of a two story stone home in Georgetown. It was cool in the summers and he had a wood burning stove to keep him warm in the winter. He could buy the wood he needed from the owner of the home above his one bedroom one bath apartment. It was perfectly located near a public transportation station. He could get anywhere in DC from this station.

Tony spent most of his time working long hours practicing law. He worked primarily on the prosecution side.

Much of his time was with his nose in books researching cases. He also spent time interviewing people for the witness stand and to gather information for the different cases that he worked on. He always sat as the second chair during trials.

In the summer of 1961, Washington got a new baseball team for the American League. The old Senators moved to Minnesota and took the name of the Twins. The Washington team kept the name of the Senators but as an expansion team under new management, they had to draft a new team from the other teams in the league. They would still play at Griffith Stadium. Mickey Vernon became their manager and they lost 101 games and only won 60. Tony was able to get to the ball park on the weekend if he wasn't out of town visiting one of the many historic sites of the area. Even though the Senators were not very good, they were entertaining. They had Jimmy Piersal playing in the outfield. He was at that time one of the most colorful players in both leagues. He hit 80 points below his normal batting average, but he was a great outfielder. Chuck Hinton lead the team with 17 home runs a .310 batting average and drove in 75 runs. Young Claude Osteen was a promising young pitcher. After going to Mass on Sunday morning, getting to downtown Griffith Stadium for an afternoon ball game was very easy. He enjoyed the warm afternoons sitting in the bleachers, eating a hot dog or two and a few cold beers. He got to see some of the best players. He made sure he got to see the New York Yankees when they came to town. Mickey Mantle and Roger Maris were chasing the Babe's home run record of 60. Getting away from the grind of the everyday life and enjoying baseball was perfect for him. It brought back the days of when he was young, when he used to go to Seals Stadium off Bryant Ave. in San Francisco and watch the Seals play in the old Pacific Coast league. He also enjoyed going by himself. He could do things at his own pace and just slow down.

If he wasn't at the ball park on the weekends, he was off by train to different towns and city's. He enjoyed Baltimore a lot. The small towns just outside of DC in Virginia we full of history and provided him with great pleasure. The summer of 61 was a great time for Tony.

As the winter began, things outside changed. No more baseball but ... Washington had a Pro football team. The Redskins. Tony really loved his football and he made sure he did not miss a game at Griffith Stadium. He fell in love with the stadium, the atmosphere and the crazy fans! He sat through all kinds of weather. Rain, sleet, snow and ice didn't stop any of the fans from coming and watching some great football. On the cold days, Tony filled a little flask full of some bourbon and poured it into his beer. They also severed real sausages, just like he made when he was working back at Allens. Nothing like a great sausage with mustard and a cold beer with bourbon while watching the great Bobby Mitchell do his thing. Norm Snead was a young quarterback who tossed 22 touchdown passes. Eleven went to Mitchell. Billy Ray Barnes was the leading rusher with 492 yards. They only won one game! Tony was hooked again on football. He loved it.

The winter from 61 into 62 was a cold one. Plenty of snow and when it didn't snow it rained. It reminded him a lot of Salem but a little more extreme. He had made some friends among his fellow lawyers but all of the men were married and they had a difficult time doing things with Tony. They spent there off time with their families. The few women that were lawyers,were really too young.

The Spring of 62 was fast approaching and in Washington D.C. The weather was always beautiful. Monument Park came alive with all of the cheery trees blossoming along the walk ways. Tony spent the third week in March walking the trails and enjoying the fresh air, the beautiful trees and people watching.

As he was sitting on a bench overlooking the Lincoln Monument, a familiar person from the prosecuting office of the local District Attorneys office sat next to him.

She smiled and started the conversation

" I usually don't sit next to strange men in the park, but I think I know you! Aren't you a Jag attorney?

This woman was blonde and very pretty. And she was smiling.

" I am" Tony replied. My name is Anthony Rucker, but you can call me Tony"

"Well, Anthony Rucker, Tony"

She paused and looked longer into brown his eyes. My name name is Rebecca Nofsinger... and you can call me Becca "

She reached her hand out and they shook hands.
They talked for what seemed like five minutes but it

was really almost and hour. They discussed the work that they do and where they had seen each other before. She was from a Augusta Maine. Which was the State Capital. Tony told her that he grew up in San Francisco. The small talk ended when Becca asked him if and when he served in the war.

"You want to walk to the Monument? Tony pointed across the long blue water of the cement pond that sits in front of the memorial.

'Sure Tony. Have you been there before?"

"Actually I have, but the walk to the Monument is something that never gets old. The tree blossoms are beautiful."

"Don't want to talk about the war ? "

"Correct. Lets keep this conversation on the happy side"

"Will do Lieutenant"

She grabbed him by his right elbow and started walking. Over her right shoulder, she had a nice brown leather purse. His mind went right to thoughts of Essa! As Rebecca looked over at Tony, she thought what a very nice smile he had.

Becca turned out to be a very interesting person with a very interesting and complicated past. Tony and her really would enjoy their time together. Because of their busy schedules, they usually only saw each other on the weekends and every once in a while at a court house. There were times when he would have a case that had the military working with the local government. Becca was a divorced parent of an eight year old daughter named Margie. Becca's ex husband lived in the D.C. area and would spend every other weekend with Margie. During the summer months Margie would spend July and August with her father.

Rebecca Nofsinger attended Georgetown Law School after graduating from the University of Maine. Washington D.C. was a whole lot different than Orono Maine and its University. In order for a woman to fit into the world of being a female lawyer, she had to be tough minded and competitive. She learned how to dress herself to look very attractive but also very professional. Becca went by Rebecca at work. She wore her blonde hair reasonably short with some strategically placed curls. Always in high heels, gave her the appearance of being tall. This helped her be able to look the men at an almost face to face level without being intimidated. She used enough makeup to give her face a memorable look that accentuated her deep blue eyes and perfect woman nose. Becca also had a small dimple on her chin. Any time she spent in the sun gave her face a very nice tanned look. Her dresses always showed off her athletic build that included small hips and an average sized looking bust. Her finger nails were always painted to match either her dress or sometimes her lip stick.

When Tony and Becca started to attend summer baseball games together on the weekends, she dressed as she did growing up. Like the Tom Boy that she really was. She loved baseball as well as football. Her knowledge of both sports was better than most men. She said her father played both sports when he was attending The University of Maine. They watched as much of each sport as possible together while she as growing up. Usually it was at the local high school and sometimes a college game or two. Becca also enjoyed drinking cold beer and eating the hot dogs and peanuts at ball games. When they didn't attend a ball game in the summer they would hop a train and visit some of the near buy places that Tony had never been too. Richmond was a great place to visit. It had so many historical places from the Civil War that they enjoyed visiting. The visit to Virginia Beach on the Chesapeake Bay was very enjoyable. They spent time walking the beach getting plenty of sun and relaxing. They also found a restaurant right on the Bay that specialized in seafood. Tony had never had lobster before! They both enjoyed some very expensive white wine.

Their weekends out of town also included some very passionate evenings. Becca was not a shy woman in the bedroom. She enjoyed showing herself to Tony and she also enjoyed Tony's body. Both had experienced their share of the opposite sex and the experiences that they would enjoy, would almost never be the same. The results of each encounter always ended with both exhausted and smiling.

They attended the last game of the Senators season against the Baltimore Orioles on a Saturday. While sitting in the stands along the third base line Tony looked at Becca and started to talk about their relationship.

"It's been a great summer Becca. Thanks."

"You say that like, you don't want it to continue?"

"Oh I do. But we need to be careful about how it will continue."

"What does that mean?"

"Well ... my past relationships didn't always end on a great note. I think I ,we, got in over our heads and I ended up not wanting what they wanted."

"And what was that?"

"Married"

Becca started to laugh then looked at Tony " I've been married once and I don't want to go through that again. You and I are great together now, but I'm sure things will change. They always do. So, lets enjoy what we have while we have it. OK?"

" That's fine with me. I'm not ready to be a step father or a husband. Who knows where my job will take me."

They raised their cups of beer and touched them together and drank from them. They both thought to themselves that this was a good decision and were happy that they talked about this. It really made for a great relationship. They could both go about their lives not worrying about what the other was doing. If they needed to spend more time at work, it was ok. If Rebecca had to spend family time with Margie and her ex, Tony would understand. This actually strengthened the relationship.

The winter of 62 came along and Tony and Rebecca

started to attend the Redskins football games.

Tony wasn't really ready for what he experienced sitting next to Rebecca!

"That was pass interference" Come on Ref!" He didn't know how passionate she was about the sport.

She enjoyed standing and cheering while waving her red and gold palm palms. The people around her enjoyed her enthusiasm and she enjoyed them. Tony was thrilled that she fit right in with those crazy Skins fans.

"Tony! We need to throw the ball more to Bobby. We can't run the ball at all." And she was always right about things. Tony usually just sat and watched the games and Becca! After the games was also fun as they would find a new restaurant to try.

After the football season ended and Christmas was behind them, Rebecca talked Tony into going skiing.

"Come on! Be adventurous! Don't be an old man!" It took some convincing but Tony actually got excited about it. Rebecca took care of all the arraignments. She booked a hotel and transportation by train to Boswell PA and The Laurel Mountain Ski Resort for the second weekend in February. They would have an extra day because it was Lincolns Birthday and government offices were closed on that Monday.

Rebecca was so excited to get away and to be skiing again. She had not been for along time.

"Tony. The last time I went skiing was in College with all of my sorority friends. We had so much fun skiing and letting the boys chase us!"

"I'll bet you guys were quite the sight. A bunch of cute snow bunnies!"

Tony had never been skiing before and he wasn't sure if he wanted Rebecca to try and teach him how. So, he paid an instructor for morning lessons on a rope tow while Rebecca went off on her own.

They met up for lunch in the lodge.

"Well ... How did it go?"

"No broken legs! It was fun but I don't think I can keep up with you! I watched you coming down the slopes. Swishing back and forth."

"Lets have a shot of tequila after lunch and head out together."

Rebecca had a big smile on her reddened face. She looked very pretty in her solid green coat and pant ski outfit. She also had a green stocking cap full of snow on her head and a pair of sun glasses to keep the glare from the snow out of her eyes. Her ski gloves matched her green outfit. Tony had a pair of black rain pants on and a rather large gray ski coat to keep him warm and dry. The sun glasses helped his eyes after he got used to them. His black ski gloves unintentionally matched his black pants. He wore a Senators baseball cap to unsuccessfully keep his head dry and warm.

The afternoon runs were difficult at first for Tony, but he was getting pretty good at going back and forth through the moguls. He also got to a point were he could jump stop. Other than a few accidents getting off of the chair lift, things went pretty good.

After getting the rentals back to the lodge, they took a shuttle bus back to the hotel, where they cleaned up and had a very nice dinner over looking the white capped mountain. After the dinner, they went to the lounge for some cocktails and dancing. The sound system in the lounge played songs like "I Can't Stop Loving You"' by Ray Charles, "The Loco Motion" by Little Eva, "Roses are Red" sung by Bobby Vinton. They both enjoyed the dry Martinis,with two olives, and the very slow dances. Tony wasn't the best at dancing without holding his partner. Becca enjoyed it when Tony would lead them in some of his west coast swing dancing. The nights music also included "Green Onions" by Booker T and The MG's, "Twist and Shout" by The Isley Brothers and of course Elvis and "Return To Sender".Some of the new songs of 1963, "Surfin U.S.A " by the Beach Boys, and "It's My Party" sung by Lesley Gore really kept the night going until closing.

After sleeping in the next morning, they had a big breakfast at the coffee shop and went back to the room to enjoy each other before getting back on the Mountain.

With the snow coming down, Tony tried to keep up with Becca who was now finding jumps to go along with the many moguls.

"You OK?" Tony had came down the hill this time first,

ahead of Becca. As he poked his head up from the snow, looking for his ski's, hat and sun glasses.

"Whew! That was actually fun!" Tony had tried to take one of the jumps Becca had been going over.

"The jump was great... but the landing needs some work." They both had a good laugh as Tony got to his feet and picked up his hat and classes.

The rest of the day was much more fun as both skiers enjoyed the cold and snowy day. The lodge was a great place to settle down and relax by being in front of the big fire place. Crab legs followed by several cold beers ending with Martini's, shaken not stirred, made for a simple dinner. They grabbed two bottles of wine, one white and one red and jumped on the shuttle bus to get back to the hotel.

Once back at their room, they opened both bottles. Tony was drinking the red, while Becca started on the white. The radio in the room was tuned into a 1940's station. So, they put the radio in the bathroom and took a long hot and steamy shower together. After getting dressed , they headed down to the hotel lounge for some BBQ-ed chicken wings and cocktails. They mixed in some dancing before heading back to the room. The train was leaving town at noon the next day.

On the trip back to D.C. Rebecca brought up the tattoos on Tony's back and the scars. He explained them and his relationship with Rich and the training they went through together. He had to tell Rebecca about how and when he lost Rich on Okinawa.

"What was it like on that island? The war?"

Tony was staring out the train window. As the scenery went by, Tony began to talk

"What I saw and did!" He paused

"No one should have to do and see."

Rebecca had never seen the expression that she was now seeing on Tony's face. It was an almost, lifeless look. It almost scared her.

"I did what I was trained to do and what I had to do to survive and to make sure my men lived on." He went on "The scars came from the hand to hand combat with

Japaneses soldiers. I'm sure those men had much to live for. I sometimes see their faces at night." Tony paused , "I hope they are resting in Peace."

The only sound, was the rhythm of the train click clacking over the tracks. There were not many people in the train car and everyone was sleeping.

"I signed up the day after Perl Harbor. It was the right thing to do. But I had no idea what I was in for. The Marine Corp has been very good for me. It got me an education and has given me the tools to have a great career. "

He turned and looked at Rebecca and said in a quiet voice

"Please don't ever ask me about that time of my life again!"

Rebecca sat in silence the rest of the way and began to wonder about the pain Tony had experienced. She would never bring it up again. Tony put his head on her shoulder and fell asleep.

Tony and Becca made it back to the Mountain one more time in March, before the ski season ended. It too, was a fantastic time. Tony was quickly learning how to navigate the moguls at higher speeds and also how to land the jumps. He also loved the work out that he got for his legs along with the evening work outs with Becca in the hotel room.

With the spring came the excitement for the up coming baseball season. Hopes were high for the Senators as a team and Tony and Becca knew they would be attending more games together. As the summer moved on to late August, Washington D.C. began to prepare for "The March on Washington". On the twenty eighth of August, over 250,000 people attended the march to protest racial discrimination and to advocate for civil and economic rights for African Americans. Tony was very interested in how all of this was to play out. D.C. had had some racial problems in the past and the city prepared for more issues as well as the large number of protesters. Tony made sure that he got to the Lincoln Memorial early enough to find a place close enough to the large make shift podium where the speakers would be. The area from the Lincoln Memorial all the way to the Washington Monument was jam packed on both sides of the long large cement pond that was in front of both majestic structures.

The high point of the day took place when Martin Luther King Jr. began to read his speech. After a few paragraphs, he went off of his written speech and began to speak from his heart. His famous words rang out " I have a Dream" and from then on everyone became captivated with his words. It became one of the greatest if not the greatest speech of the civil rights era. This speech put great pressure on then President John F. Kennedy to sign a bill to end segregation and ensure equal employment opportunities for all people. The bill would eventually be signed later by President Lyndon Johnson.

Having served with many different ethnic groups, Tony thought he understood what the lives of the poor and non white folks was like. Over then next few weeks,the more he listened to those who protested and to those who lived those lives, the more he found out that he didn't know much. He found out that what you see from afar isn't what you really think. An example that was pointed out to him by an African American who worked at the court house was.

" Take just the simple act of walking home. You never have to worry about being stopped by the police, because they didn't stop white people. If you are black and in a white neighborhood, you would be stopped by police. And if you said the wrong thing or acted indifferent you could be beaten and taken to jail."

Those issues along with segregation of schools and neighborhoods along with other civil rights became more important to Tony. It was a wake up call to him who, like most whites, had been living in a different world than all minorities.

He really wasn't sure how this would affect him, but he knew that he would have to make changes in how he looked at things and more importantly, how he reacted to situations.

In early November, Tony was called into see the General in charge of the Jag program. He hadn't been to Quantico Virginia for a while.

"Lieutenant Rucker, good to see you again" Tony saluted General Dykes and he saluted back. The General pointed to a chair for Tony to sit as he sat behind his desk.

"Lieutenant .. You know that within The Corp movement is always a possibility as is promotions. You have done a fine job here in Washington D.C. And are ready to move to another situation so that we can use your experience and abilities."

"Yes Sir, I understand." Tony knew that he was going to be ordered to move to another location. Before he arrived at Quantico, he was given a heads up by his present commanding officer.

"You will have a choice." The General looked a two sets of orders on his desk.

"The first... is a position in our new office in South Vietnam. Are you familiar with the location?"

"Yes Sir I am." Tony had been staying up with the activity that was going on there. He figured that the assignment would be in Saigon, the Capital city.

"The other choice is across the country to your old neck of the woods, south of San Francisco."

General Dykes explained both assignments in detail. The conversation lasted over an hour. Tony was told to think things over and have a decision tomorrow. It wasn't much time to decide, but it was an easy one. He wanted to go back home. He for sure didn't want to live over seas again especially in the climate that he would be enduring in Saigon.

Tony would be leaving the first of December. He had two weeks to get things in order before leaving. Tony knew that his conversation and the last fifteen day with Rebecca would be difficult as well as memorable.

The weekend of Friday the 20th of November was the weekend that Margie would spend with her father. Tony met Rebecca at a very nice Italian restaurant downtown Washington D.C. After they both got off of work at 6:00. They had cocktails in the bar while they waited for a seat. They talked about work that week and finally sat down for dinner. The waiter poured Tony a portion of the wine that they ordered for him to sample.

"That will work Mario!"

Mario, their usual waiter, poured both a class of the red Claret.

Tony looked at Rebecca, smiled and said
" I have something to tell you."

"You look serious! Is it?"

"You remember our conversation at the baseball game when you said this would not last for ever?"

Rebecca put her class down and looked right into Tony's eyes

A long drown out "Yes?"

"I was given the choice of my next assignment." he had a short pause as Rebecca tilted her pretty face to the side with a questioned look.

" I'm being promoted to Captain and transferred to the San Francisco area. I'll have my own command at the Navel base just South of the City."

"Tony, I'm very proud of you. I knew it would happen sooner than later. You are an outstanding attorney." She also paused before saying "I'm going to really miss you and all of our adventures. When do you leave?"

Tony was somewhat surprised at her response but also thankful. They both understood that this would be their last weekend together. Thanksgiving was the next Thursday and she and Margie would be at her parents home in Maine and Tony would be getting his things together to leave. They crabbed a taxi after dinner and went to her home for the evening. They had a bottle of wine and listened to her stereo and even danced little. They spent most of the night exploring and enjoying each other. Saturday was spent at the memorials walking along the paths and sitting at the bench where they met. The talked about what might happen in the future for each, as well as remembering all of the good times that they had together. Tony had never been to an Opera, so Rebecca and Tony dressed to the nines did dinner and drinks and went to the three act Operetta. They took advantage of there last night and morning together at Rebecca's home. They were both very sad and when the cab arrived in front of her home, they had their final long hug, tears came from both of their eyes as they kissed.

"Go Redskins!" Rebecca then waved as Tony got into the back seat.

Tony was on a Navy transport flight to San Francisco on the 27th of November 1964.

CHAPTER TWELVE

Tony's move back to "The City" and bay area, was an easy transition. His parents no longer lived in Butchertown. They had moved South down the peninsula about twenty five miles to the little town of San Bruno. Butchertown was no longer the mixed community that it had been in the 20's and 30's. After the second war ended, many of the African Americans who had migrated to the area to build ships at Hunters Point Ship Yard, liked the area and stayed. Many continued to live in the Hunters Point Public Housing that was used to provide places to live for the workers. Many of these families were joined by other family members from the South and bought up most of the other housing in the area. In the Northern part of Butchertown, near the creek, The slaughter houses and the businesses that supported them had bought up most of the property and built larger and modern facilities. They also needed the room to corral all of the animals that were now being trucked into the area. Butchertown no longer seemed like a safe place to live. San Bruno and the small towns South of San Francisco where very quite and with newly built homes and neighborhoods.

The area also became the center of activity of the newly founded Black Panther Party. This was formed in Oakland to help improve the lives of African Americans. Civil Rights around the country was a major movement and this was the area in San Francisco where most of the activity took place. The Hunters Point/Butchertown area also became home to the San Francisco Giants. The Major league baseball team had moved to "The City" in 1959 and built a new stadium in Candlestick Cove called Candlestick Park. The new stadium was located close to the Housing Projects.

Tony settled into the Navel Housing buildings at the San Bruno Navel Base. By the middle of December, Tony had become somewhat at home in his one bedroom apartment on the Base. The South exit to the Base was within three miles of his parents house on Cypress. What few possessions Tony had, fit nicely in his officers apartment, which came furnished.

That first week on Base, was used to familiarize himself with the base and his responsibilities at the JAG office. As a Captain, now he would be the lead prosecuting attorney on many of the cases. Major Steve Cooper would be the commanding officer. "Coop" as Tony would call him when not in the office,was younger than Tony. He had gone directly to OCS and TBS right out of college after graduating from high school. They would spend much of their off time together running and working out. Coop was taller than Tony and a little quicker. Tony had a thicker build and was a little stronger. Coop was also a stand up guy. No nonsense, fair and a great sense of humor. Coop was the youngest of three boys growing up off the coast of North Carolina. The boys and father spent all of their free time fishing the rivers or in the mountains hunting for deer and elk. He also liked to drink beer, which Tony also enjoyed.

The Rucker family celebrated Christmas by attending Saint Roberts Catholic Church at the morning Mass. The church was located right next to the City Park of San Bruno. Tony's brothers , Robert and Paul and their families, joined his sister Joyce at his parents home on Cypress. They enjoyed opening presents, a late lunch followed by a late ham dinner with all of the trimmings. Everyone wanted to hear about Tony's time in Washington D.C. He told stories about the crazy football fans, the cold and snowy weather and about all of the monuments. He also talked about his trips to many of the historical sights in Virginia that he had visited.

The Base office would be closed until Thursday the second of January. Tony took advantage of no one being in the office, as he worked by himself getting organized and caught up on the cases he would be working on. On Tuesday, the thirty first, Tony had dinner at a local restaurant on the old highway number One or as it was called, The El Camino. It was the main road that went through all of the little towns going South to San Jose. He sat down to dinner at The El Rancho Hotel restaurant. It had a large bar that had a window looking into the hotels rather large swimming pool. Tony enjoyed the time by himself. After finishing dinner by 6:00, he stopped at a Mom and Pops store to pick up a bottle of Merlot. He then drove North on the Bayshore freeway to the Broadway exit on his way to Coit Tower. It had been twenty five years since he and Janessa had spent a wonderful night together there. He had always wondered what had happened to her and if she would show up tonight. He had been there several times on New Years Eve thinking she might be there but never saw her.

Tony normally didn't dress in his uniform, but for this one night, he thought it would be ok. He pulled into the parking lot in his old Ford. His parents had held on to that for all of these years..He was using it until he could get around to buying something new and more reliable.

At that very same time, Janessa left Francis and Katy at her next door neighbors home.

"Not sure how long I'll be. Probably not very long."

Janessa also stopped for a bottle of Chardonnay to go along with two small plastic cups she had in the trunk of her car. Just maybe, she thought. This time he will show up. The drive to Coit Tower was only ten minutes. When she arrived in the parking lot, she recognized the old Ford. She sat for a few seconds to compose herself, crabbed the wine and glasses, then approached the car and Tony. He was sitting with his back to her on the hood of the Ford.

Without a sound, Tony felt a rather hard punch to his left shoulder. As he turned, he stared right into Janessa's beautiful eyes.

"Why didn't you call me? She smiled with that sheepish smile and tilted head. Tony replied

"I forgot your number!"

"Not a good excuse soldier."

"How can I make it up to you, my fair maiden?"

'Well..." Janessa held up the bottle of Chardonnay and two glasses

"Join me at the top of the tower!"

"Yes mam." He came to attention, but did not salute

As they took the elevator to the observation deck, They didn't say a word. They just were thinking how each was so lucky that the other made it to this place again at the same time.

After Janessa pored each a glass of the white wine, they began to talk just as though they had never parted ways. They laughed a lot talking about "old times".That was followed by brief updates about their lives.

Tony could not believe how wonderful she looked. She was no longer a teenager, but the most attractive woman he had ever seen. How could she be more beautiful than when she was younger? But she was.

She to looked at him in wonderment. My, she thought, look what he has turned into. Tall, dark and very handsome.

The uniform gave him an added look of professionalism. His face still looked the same, but the boyish look had turned into a man. A very attractive one.

They both noticed that even though they had both aged and matured some, the personalities were still the same. They both could feel an excitement that they hadn't had for a very long time. Both could not stop smiling.

Time was flying by. They started on the second bottle of Merlot and kept talking. Mid night came around and a night watchman in his blue uniform came by and asked them to please leave and that he was closing up the tower for the evening.

"Wow! As always with you, it seems as though we could talk for ever!" Janessa looked at Tony with her sly smile. "But I do need to get home to my two kids."

" I get it." Tony took her by her arm and escorted her down to the parking lot and then to her car. "I would like to call you and see you again soon. Would you give me your pone number?"

"I never give out my number to Marines. But in this case, I will make an exception." Again her soft looking lips formed a beautiful sheepishly sly smile.

Tony took both of her warm hands in his, raised them up and kissed her long fingers. "I'll call you. When is a good time?"

"After seven any evening."

Tony opened the door to her car and she got in and rolled down the window. As she drove away she smiled again and she said "After seven" waved and drove off.

Tony spent the next day at his parents house and watched the 49th Rose Bowl between Number one ranked Southern Cal and number two ranked Wisconsin. Janessa also watched the game from her living room. She was a big football fan and would not miss the most important College football game of the season.

Tony called Janessa from his apartment on the Base at 7:01!

After saying their hello's, Janessa almost yelled into the phone" Did you watch the Rose Bowl today?" Without giving Tony time to answer, Janessa excitingly said " Great finish! Wisconsin came storming back in that last quarter. If they get that onside kick, they would have pulled it off. 44-42!"

Tony got a quick "But they didn't."

It was past twelve when they finally got off the phone. Both so excited neither could hardly sleep.

They took turns calling each other that week and made plans to meet for dinner on Saturday night.

Tony had made reservations for two at Alioto's Restaurant at Fisherman's Wharf. He requested a table for two that over looked the wharf. Tony arrived first and sat in the Bar for a cocktail. Bomb

Bay Gin Martini shaken with two olives. Tony was casually dressed with a sport coat covering a light blue polo shirt and black slacks and his favorite cowboy boots. Janessa walked gracefully in just after Tony. She sat next to him at the Bar without him seeing her.

"Hay sailor, Buy a girl a drink?" Tony turned to her " Not sure I know you! But Ok. What will ya have?"

She looked at the bartender "I'll have what he's having." She was wearing in a long Brown wool coat that covered her long darker brown sleeveless dress. Around her neck was a Saint Christopher medal that hung four inches. She had matching high heels that showed off her nicely shaped calves. It was and interesting but classy look. The little make up that she wore brought out her brown eyes and soft lips. She looked not only attractive but beautiful. Every one turned their head when she walked in, except Tony!

Their table became ready about the time that they had finished their Martinis. They followed the Mature d to the dimly lit table that overlooked the fishing boats that were docked at the wharf. The Mature D pulled the chair for Janessa and she easily sat down.

The waiter gave Tony a wine list. " You my friend, should make this order. I don't often drink fancy wine."

'I think I'll wait until we order." She looked at the waiter. But we will have two Boom Bay Gin Martinis with two olives."

Tony laughed "You know your Gin!"

"No. I just took a guess." She smiled with that sly look that really got to Tony.

They both ordered Nonna Rosa's Crab Cioppono and a side order of the homemade sausage for their dinners. Janessa also bought a bottle of the Chardonnay that the waiter suggested .

After the very romantic dinner they sat outside under cover from the drizzle on a bench facing the inner bay that was lit up beautifully. They talked for awhile and decided to head over to Union Square and the Saint Francis Hotel. Tony called a cab from the phone both.

Once inside they went to the lounge for some dancing and a cocktail. During a very slow dance while they were holding each other, Janessa looked up into Tony's eyes and smiled her smile. Tony leaned down and softly kissed her. The excitement that the little kissed caused between the two of them went right through both of their bodies. They finished the dance without saying anything.

They finally left the Saint Francis in the backseat of a Yellow cab and headed back to their cars at the wharf. Janessa snuggled into Tony's arms for the ride. Once at their cars, Tony stood with Janessa outside of her car. She thanked him for the wonderful evening and then they enjoyed a very long kiss.

The couple began to date as often as possible. Tony had also enrolled at the University of San Francisco Law School to study Criminal Law. The accelerated course would take him two years to complete. This would allow him to become promoted to a Major. He wasn't sure if he would be transferred upon completion to another duty. With that degree he would also be eligible to command any billet in the Marine Corps. He had heard rumors that military action in the little country of South Vietnam could be picking up some. He wouldn't be to excited to be deployed there. But he had to continue his education if he wanted to be promoted to higher ranks.

Tony and Janessa would spend many hours talking about his future in the Corp and how it would affect their relationship. Tony had Janessa had spent 25 years apart and both didn't want that to happen again.

Tony also knew that he would have twenty years in the Marine Corp in 1969, which was five years away and he could retire in 1974.

CHAPTER THIRTEEN

Tony's weekdays were very long days. He would attend class until noon every day at The University of San Francisco's Law School. He would then drive back to the Navy Base in San Bruno, which was about forty five minutes depending on traffic. Tony would finish the day at around 6:00 every night depending on the work load. Trying to find time to study and get a work out in was difficult. He would get up buy 5:00 every morning for a run and some weight training on the base. He made sure that he called Janessa every night at 7:01. The conversation usually ended around 9 to 9:30 so that he could get some time with the books.

Janessa also stayed busy at work and shuttling the

kids around to their different activities. Both Francis and Katy were playing basketball after school as well as Cub Scouts for Francis and Girl Scouts for Katy. The weekends were set aside for the four of them to go do different activities together. Tony and the children got along very well. He made sure that they knew that he wasn't trying to take their fathers place, but he was very interested in all of the things that they were involved in.

The beginning of May were his final exams. He would have a three week break before the summer session started. Tony and Janessa both took a Friday off, left the children with the neighbor and drove to Lake Tahoe for a couple of days. Tony had bought himself a 1962 Chevy Impala. It was a reliable blue four door sedan. With its Three on the tree transmission and a 327 cubic inch V eight engine, it had plenty of power. They took Hwy 80 to Sacramento and then Hwy 50 to South Lake Tahoe.

On the ride to Sacramento, Essa asked Tony about what he had done when he first left the Marines. Tony spent time talking about his time on Maui. How he needed to "get away" from life and without any responsibilities.

"Life was good on the island. Great weather and a simple life. I made friends with two brothers, Willie and Kemo. They taught me how to surf. We spent all of our free time on the beach and in the ocean. They also introduced me to the Hawaiian life and "Hawaiian time." When describing Keke he talked with respect. "She was a very young and inquisitive woman. We talked about life on the main land."

"I thought a lot about what I wanted to do in life while

I was swimming in the ocean and sitting on the beach. That's when I decided that I wanted to go to college, play football and become a lawyer."

"Why Salem Oregon? Essa asked

"Rich was from Bend Oregon and he talked about playing baseball after the war for a small school in Salem called Willamette. It just so happened that it had a football team and a Law School. I also knew that I could not be around you while you were still with Brad."

"Salem is a nice little town. I could be who I wanted to be without people asking questions. I could, most of the time, forget about the War and the things I saw and did."

"What about those things Anthony? What did you see and do?"

Tony quickly changed the conversation back to Salem.

"I enjoyed playing football. It was fun and I met many great young guys. I was "The old man." He laughed at that.

"I heard that you had a very pretty girl friend and that you were very serious about her. You even brought her to The City."

"Her name was Amara. She worked in the canary where I worked. We spent a lot of time together and we were very serious about getting married."

"Why didn't you two get married?"

"It really came down to my decision to get back into the Marines. In order to get my law degree without cost, I would go through the process of OCS and TBS in Quantico. That took a year and I would follow that with Law School in DC." He paused for a bit while down shifting and making a turn on to Hwy 50.

"She didn't like the separation and the wait. She got married. Plus, she wasn't you."

Tony went on to describe many of the sights that he saw in DC and in the states near. He finally told her about Becca.

"Becca was a lot of fun. She was divorced and would never get married again. Our relationship was always going to be temporary. She too was a layer, but in the private sector and knew that after three years I would be transferred somewhere. And I did."

Janessa asked a lot of questions about Hawaii,Salem and Virginia. Tony was very open with Essa about his past, with the exception of his time in the Marine Corp before and during the War. He would avoid any question about what he called "dark times".

Hwy 50 was a very windy road that was mostly one lane each way. Tony carried chains in the trunk because it always had a chance of snowing. The drive took close to six hours as they stopped in the old mining town of Placerville for lunch.

After leaving Placerville they continued their conversation, this time things turned to Janessa. Tony really didn't want to know details about her long relationship with Brad. As she began to talk about Brad Tony broke in

"Ya know Essa, I know Brad and I saw what went on while I was around. What happened there is over and I really don't want to know anything about him or your time together. I hope that doesn't hurt your feelings."

"Actually, I really don't want to talk about that time of my life. It was a long time ago and I was just trying to figure things out. I will say that I always worried about you and what was going on with you in your life."

"I did decide to get my life in order after that break up. I concentrated on finishing school and finding some kind of job where I could show not only myself but others that I could be successful in the business world. I worked hard at school and I put many long extra hours at work."

"Knowing what I know about you, it would have been fun and impressive watching you go about your business. I'm very proud of what you have accomplished."

Janessa began to talk about her marriage and why things just feel apart. Tony found that very interesting.

"Anthony, you also need to know that when I gave birth to Katy, there were complications with the birth."

"What happened?"

It was difficult for Tony to concentrate on his driving and also listen to Essa. They were getting to the summit on Hwy 50 and it was a very narrow winding one lane road. A guard rail on the right was the only thing from keeping the car from going over a very steep cliff.

" I had some complications with the birth. I had a C section. The doctor told Richard and I that he didn't think I would be able to have any more children."

"How did you deal with that?

"I have been OK with it. With the divorce, I really only cared abut taking great care of the kids. Having another never really crossed my mind."

She paused "until now."

They both discussed what happened and how it would be like going forward. Tony admitted to Essa that he was surprised but as long as she was healthy and that the children that she did have were happy and healthy, things would be just fine.

The drive down the mountain was much safer. The Tahoe Basin, even though it was still above 6,200 feet above sea level, was warm and beautiful. With the windows open, the fresh smell of the Pine and Fir trees was very soothing.

They arrived at the Stateline and Harvey's Hotel and Casino at 3:00 in the afternoon. Stateline was the area where Nevada and California came together along Hwy 50. Their room on the seventh floor overlooked the Lake from a balcony. At 3:30 in the afternoon, the sun made the deep lake a very dark blue. With no wind on the lake it appeared to be very still. They couldn't see any boats on the the large body of water but a little two seat plane was gliding low over the chrystal clear water.

"The view from that plane is probably spectacular." Janessa just stared at the lake from the balcony. Tony came up from behind and wrapped his hands around her waste, and kissed her on the neck.

Lake Tahoe sits at the bottom of the basin of the Sierra Nevada Mountains at 6,225 feet above sea level. It is also the second deepest lake in the United States at over 1,600 feet. Its vast shoreline covers 191 square miles of Pine and Fir forests

"After that long ride, why don't we go for a swim in the lake! Its walking distance, no wind and still 80 degrees out."

"Sounds like a great idea. I'll get into my suit and we can grab a few towels." Janessa didn't take her eyes off of the vast beautiful blue lake.

Janessa headed into the bathroom to change and Tony pulled on his long swim suit. It had been a long time since he had been on a beach and he was really looking forward to getting into the water to cool off and relax.

Once they found a nice spot on the sandy beach, Tony spread out a large towel he got from the hotels front desk. He also grabbed two lawn chairs to sit in. After taking off their shoes, they found out that the sand was very hot. Tony took off the white tee shirt he was wearing and exposed his very muscular upper body. For the first time Janessa saw the tattoos on his back and the scars that he had from his time fighting in the jungles.

"I'll race you to the water!" Tony was like a little kid.

"No, you go ahead. I'm going to stay for a bit and lay out. "

"Ok. Suit yourself."

Tony sprinted to the water. His feet hit the freezing cold water at a full sprint. Three or four strides into the water he dove out and went under the water. It was then that he realize how cold the mountain lake water really was. It was shocking but also very refreshing. He swam out to a floating wooded dock and pulled himself up on the dock and stood tall. He looked down into the water and could see the bottom. It had some very large boulders that sat on top of the sandy floor. He wondered how deep it was. He could also see the chain that was attached to the dock holding it in place and where it was hooked to the bottom of the lake. For the fun of it , Tony dove in to see how deep it really was, and swam to the bottom. He counted to twenty five before he reached the hooked up chain. It was so clear and beautiful. He saw several curious trout swim by him, before he slowly swam to the top and rested on the dock. After becoming dry while laying on the dock, Tony dove in and swam to the beach. Janessa met him at the water line as she walked out to waist high in the water to cool off.

"So what do those tattoos represent?"

"Kind of a long story."

" Are they related to your time over seas?"

Anthony and Janessa had really never talked about his time in the Marines or any of the action that he had seen while in the war. She could tell that he tried to put many of those times behind him, but she was very interested.

"I know you don't like to talk about your time serving, but its so much of a big part of your life, I think if you told me some things I would be able to understand you better."

"You are probably right."

They both looked out over the vast blue waters of Lake Tahoe that was surrounded by the snow covered mountains formed in the Ice Age and the vast forests. Standing in the water, Tony explained the two tattoos on his back. He finished the story with,

"Scriv and I were pretty tight. We were so much alike it was scary. We spent months together training and preparing for what was ahead of us." Tony paused

"He would say "We ain't going to fear anything because we have each other. We got each others back. We will fight are ass off knowing we are going to dye."

"And dam he did."

"When I saw the hole in his head, I wanted to stop and

cry. But I also knew that I had to go on."

"Rich knew deep down, that he wasn't going to survive the war."

" I had to finish for the both of us."

Janessa took his hand in hers and they both slowly walked back to the chairs on the beach.

"I'm sure Rich would be very proud of you."

"Essa, I would like to tell you some of my experiences, but not up hear at this beautiful place. War is so disgusting, dirty and sad, I want to enjoy our time here."

"Being here with you, helps me forget all of the ugliness. Let's just have fun, and enjoy each other."

"Deal"

Janessa gave Tony her famous smile and reached up and placed her smooth lips on his.

"That's more like it. " Tony smiled

The two made it back to their room and cleaned themselves up and headed down to the main floor of the casino and found one of the nice restaurants to eat dinner.

After dinner they walked through the casino to see what it had to offer. The gaming room was very large with eight black jack tables that had minimum bets as low as $2 and as much as $25. It also had four crap tables with minimum bets as low as $1 and as high as $10. It was surrounded by slot machines and other games. It was also very loud. Cocktail waitress's seemed to be every where. They usually wore low cut tops and very high skirts! Security guards also seemed to be every where. They usually were very big men dressed in green uniforms.

Tony and Essa sat at a pair of quarter slot machines and began to play. It wasn't long before a waitress came by to get there free cocktail orders. Essa ordered a glass of white wine and Tony a bottle of beer. The slots were fun to play and paid out fairly well but no big Jack Pots. After an hour, They both made it over to a $2 black jack table. Essa really enjoyed playing "21" . Tony had fun because he was with Essa, but really wanted to play craps.

One middle aged man sat next to Essa and began to play two hands at once using 100 dollar bills. Soon two of the green dressed security guards stood behind him with the Pit Boss. The Pit Boss watched two hands played then tapped the man playing the $100 bills on the shoulder and asked him to follow the guards.

Essa looked at the dealer and asked "Whats up with that guy?"

The dealer smiled and said "Those were fake bills."

"What's going to happen to him?"

At the same time the two guards opened the front doors with the man's face.

"Oh. The casino staff will have a "talk" with him. It won't be pleasant. Then they will call the police"

The dealer continued "We don't like that around here!' She laughed. "We like to show people what happens when they try to steal from us." Blood from the mans face was left on the glass door for a reminder to everyone.

After several free cocktails and some Black Jacks, Essa looked at Tony and said "It's been a long day Tony and we have much to do tomorrow. Lets head up to the room." Tony was itching to get on the crap table but agreed. He was tired also.

Tony opened the door to their seventh floor room and followed Essa in. They both went to the balcony that over looked Lake Tahoe and its full night time beauty. The partially full moon radiated light off of the very still water. A few seconds passed and they turned and faced each other. Together they met each others lips in a very passionate kiss. Tony held Essa by her hips with his two hands and she wrapped her arms under his arms and up to the small of his back. She parted her lips and began to explore Tony's mouth with her tongue. Tony returned the favor. Neither had had this type of felling since they were together in high school.

Essa pulled back after some time and looked at Tony

Waving her hand in front of her face as if to cool herself off.

"Wow! That brings back some pleasant memories

with you!"

"Sure did"

Essa grabbed his hand and with a squeeze "I think I'll get ready for bed." She turned and made her way to the bathroom.

Tony pulled over a chair from the near by table and pulled his shirt off and sat so he could take in the view of the late night lake and mountains.

It was very soon that Essa walked out of the bathroom wearing a nice silk reddish pink robe. It came to her elbows and just above her mid thighs. She looked stunning. The front was tied loosely open exposing parts of her chest and stomach. Her long hair was pulled up, showing her smooth neck and ears.

"Anthony. Will you join me?"

"I think I will"

Tony walked over to the side of the bed where Essa was standing. He removed the white shorts he was wearing exposing himself to Essa. He reached out and untied the robe. It fell to the floor revealing Essa's slight but curvy body. They came to each other and resumed their previous kiss as they pressed against each others warm bodies.

Not having to worry about becoming pregnant and wanting to fully enjoy these moments and night, they nestled into each others arms on the cool white sheets.

While looking into each others eyes Essa and Tony kissed and began to trust each other. Tony became very sensitive to every breath and movement Essa made. Essa completely gave her body to Tony and her mind fully enjoyed what was happening. She, without knowing, moved her body with every one of Tony's movements and would change her breathing as Tony touched her with his hands, lips and tongue. Essa would wispier to Tony "Yes" or "More". He understood that each woman was different, and that they reached orgasms in different ways and with different rhythms. He wanted to make sure that Essa would have so much pleasure, that she would want to continue making love with Tony.

They both woke up in the morning knowing that they had never enjoyed themselves so much. Tony's expectations of what it might be like to make love to Essa were defiantly met. In fact they were well over his expectations. She too, was overly pleased with what happened during the night. They talked about what happened and if possible could it be better.

"Not that I think it can, but I think we owe it to ourselves Anthony to see if we can do better!' Janessa smiled that unusual smile at Tony.

"I would have to agree with you."

They enjoyed each other for some time in the bed in the morning and openly without concern, talked to each other about little movements and positions that they each enjoyed. They then decided to shower together and and explore each other more before getting ready for the day.

After the morning brunch, the two drove to Zephre Cove, which was twenty minutes along highway 50 towards the North Shore of the Lake. The Cove had a nice little lodge that sat back in the tall Pine trees away from the Lake about half a mile. It included a pier that reached out into Lake Tahoe and was the home to "Miss Dixie" a paddle wheel boat that toured the lake. For a minimal price, they boarded Miss Dixie for the noon tour. The ride on Lake Tahoe took about three hours. It included a trip to Emerald Bay and the old castle that sat on a little island in the Bay. The tour guide had many stories and information about the Lake and its formation, its mysteries and legends. Both Essa and Anthony enjoyed the warm sun and the cooling breeze. They also could not get over how clear and clean the water was. They also enjoyed some cold ham sandwiches and several glasses of red and white wine.

After the Miss Dixie tour, the couple found that Zepher Cove also had a very large horse stable. Feeling adventurous, they decided to rent a couple of horses and went along a trail ride that included a trip into the woods and along the beach. By the late afternoon, they were both a little tired. Essa decided to take a nap and Tony went down to the near by beach to get some sun and time in the water. Later they drove South along highway 50 10 minutes to an area called Bijou for a quite dinner in a small Italian restaurant that sat facing Lake Tahoe. The restaurant also included a small lounge. The dance floor was made of very old wood and had been there for years. It was very different from anything Essa had seen in San Francisco, but was a lot like some of the taverns Tony had been to in Oregon. Both being tired from the long day and a little soar from the horseback ride, they decided to get some sleep.

The morning started with Essa and Tony enjoying each other. It was very nice because they could take their time, rest and talk about what the future might have in store for them.

After breakfast in the Casino dinner, they made their way to the beach with a couple chairs and a cooler of cold beer. They also had two sandwiches made and put those in the cooler for lunch. They both spent time in the cold lake water and on the dock. Essa enjoyed diving into the water to cool off and to swim to the bottom. Tony had never kissed anyone in twenty feet of cold water before, but he sure enjoyed doing it with Essa!She did too!

Sitting close too each other on the beach, they were surrounded by many other couples and kids playing and enjoying the weekend.

Tony then spent much of the time talking about his time on Okinawa.

"You lose all feeling or care for anything. The lose of life is all around you. You could actually smell it!All I could do was make sure that my guys stayed safe but at the same time advance. It was kill or be killed. A savage way of thinking. For a long time, I would see the faces of those I killed in my dreams. I would also see the faces of my guys who didn't come back. Rich!"

While talking to Essa, he very seldom looked at her. He just starred at the surrounding mountains and the calm lake water. When he talked , tears began to rolled down his cheeks. His voice was just loud enough for Essa to hear.

He was not sure about telling Essa about what he saw,but she insisted.

"The smell and sight of the burning bodies was at first difficult but I got used to it. Being surrounded by the crap and maggot infested bodies became an all of the time occurrence. It all just gives you a numb feeling. Day after wet day. You forget what day it is, you don't care."

Tony went on to explain his lack of relationships with his fellow soldiers.

"I just didn't want to get close to them. I lost Rich and that really hurt. I didn't want to hurt like that again. I also had to make decisions about who did what. Most of those decisions would put soldiers in bad spots but it had to be done. I didn't or could not do what was right if I cared about them as friends. I know they all hated me."

"Anthony .... were you scared at all during your time on those islands?"

"Without a doubt. All of the time, but somehow you could not let that effect what you did or how you did it. After living in fear for so long, you almost become numb. I had to fight that. Fear kept me sharp."

Essa asked many other questions about his training and his time on Okinawa. Tony did not tell her about his killing of others while in hand to hand combat.

"So, you can see why when I came home I had to get to a place where I could try to put that time behind me. In Hawaii, no one asked me about "What I did in the War".

They finished the beer and sandwiches and got one last swim to the dock and several under water kisses before heading South back towards The Bijou in the blue Chevy. They had noticed a Pee Wee golf course on the side of the road the night before and decided to get in "A Round."

"Now that was fun." Essa started to laugh and pointed at Tony

" I beat you by one stroke! Tony replied "Next year I want a rematch!"

"You're on!"

They had to hustle back to the hotel to shower and change or else they would have played that course one more time. Tony had made reservations at the Cal Neva Club on the North Shore for dinner and the show. Performing in the ballroom that evening was Frank Sinatra. Essa was really excited.

The drive took forty five minutes around the lake. The Cal Neva Club was located on the California Nevada stateline on the North side of the lake. There is two other Casinos with hotels close to The Cal Neva. The Crystal Bay Club was next door up a little hill and The Biltmore was on the other side of highway 50. The highway was a one lane road in each direction that encircled the lake. The big bar inside of The Cal Neva over looked Lake Tahoe. The huge window covered almost the entire length of the back of the building. Part of it was in both states! The walls of the Casino where covered with old barn wood, giving it a very old look. It also had several Elk heads on the walls and a very large stuffed Black Bear stood in a corner growling and showing its large claws.

They took their seats in the ballroom. They sat in the second level with another couple in a curved padded pink booth that closed them in. It gave them some privacy from the rest of the room. They ordered their dinner and listened to the band before Frank Sinatra took the main stage. The waiter placed a bill in front of the other couple but did not present one to Tony.

Tony asked the waiter "Where is my bill Sir?"

"Your bill has been taken care of Sir."

"But by who?"

"The gentleman who paid for your evening Sir will meet you after the show right here."

"What's going on Anthony?"

"I'm not sure, but someone paid for our dinner."

Sinatra walked on to the stage holding a mic in his hand to some background music. When the music paused Frank opened with.

"How did all of these people get into my room?"

He continued on with a very funny 4 minute mono log before breaking into "Just the Way You Look Tonight"

Sinatra captivated the audience for two hours. He knew how to entertain people by mixing his songs and music with stories and jokes.

When the house lights came on everyone slowly worked their way out of the ballroom and into the Casino. Tony and Essa sat and talked waiting for the mystery person who took care of things for them.

The man walked towards them in a black tuxedo. He had a very familiar walk, like a Marine. He was bald and short but stout. He looked uncomfortable in the tuxedo.

He saluted and said "Gunny Rucker!"

"Pardini?"

"Yes Sir" He broke his serious face and broke into a big smile. Tony got up and walked to Pardini. They silently hugged each other and tears came to their eyes. Essa smiled and began to also cry with happiness.

"Pardini what the fuck are you doing here?"

Pardini explained that he was working for Sinatra as a body guard. He had grown up in the same neighborhood in Jersey that Sinatra did and knew him when he was a kid.

"Frank heard I was out of the Marines after the war and I needed a job. So, we talked and I've been with him ever since. I travel everywhere with him."

"Essa.. I want you to meet Pete Pardini, we served together on Okinawa"

"Gunny, I didn't know you knew my first name!"

"It's Tony.... Pete. All that other stuff is behind us know"

They talked for a brief minute as Tony thanked him for the dinner.

"You have some time Tony?"

"Yes. Whats up?"

" Follow me"

They walked back towards the stage and down some steps an into a large under ground walk way.
The three began to walk down a long lighted tunnel.

"Where are we going Pete?"

Pete explained that under the casino and hotel that there was a tunnel system that led to different bungalows and different parts of the hotel.

They finally came to a large door and walked through it. It then opened up into a very large room that overlooked a small beach with Lake Tahoe in the background. There were several people seated at a rather large table preparing for a dinner. The room had a nice well stocked bar and a bartender dressed in a white tuxedo. Several well dressed waitresses were moving around the room as a sixteen speaker hidden stereo system played some soothing music.

"Whats this Pete? We don't belong here!"

"Oh yes you do. I saw you sitting in the audience before the show started and told Frank that you were here. He insisted that you come to the after show dinner and party. He was the one who took care of your bill, not me! He wants to meet you and Essa."

Sinatra came out of his room and walked right up to Pete, Tony and Essa.

"Pete here, told me all about you Gunny." and shook his hand."He said you were the baddest of all of the bad ass fighters. You often took on the most dangerous jobs to protect others. What you did for your guys and Pete here, makes my heart proud to be with you. It was guys like you and Pete that got us through an offal time. Thank You."

"Thank you Mr. Sinatra. I was just doing my job."

"It's Frank. And bull shit, you went beyond your job."

Tony introduced Essa to Frank. He took her hand and kissed the back of it "You are, without a doubt, part Italian." He was so polite and charming that Essa could hardly talk and blushed before she hit him on the shoulder.

With a smile he said" Pete .. we got a live one here" They all smiled and laughed. Frank wanted to know what

Tony was doing these days and was impressed when he heard that he was a Jag Lawyer and told him "If you retire from the Corps , look me up! I need tough, hard working lawyers I can trust working for me."

Everyone sat down when Frank did and the party started. After dinner people began to dance and Frank asked Essa for several dances Eventually, Essa and Tony made it back to their car and Pete gave Tony his phone number.

"Frank is serious about you working for him. We will stay in touch Tony". They gave each other a hug and Pete also hugged Essa as they got into the car for the drive to the Hotel.

Neither one could believe what had transpired that evening. They talked like little kids on the drive back. Tony was just so happy that he and Pete could now become friends. They had shared so much together and had so much in common. They would make an effort to find the others in their little platoon. It would take some effort, but they would get it done.

CHAPTER FOURTEEN

Knowing that it would be a while before they would not have the type of time together that they had just had, Essa and Anthony woke up early to enjoy themselves one last time before heading home. Holding hands like a young couple, they also took a short walk down to the near by beach to get one last look at the beautiful blue calm waters of Lake Tahoe. Their conversation was again about Frank and the after party in his private bungalow.

With breakfast in them, they loaded the Chevy and headed back on to the one lane high way 50 towards Sacramento and what they called reality. Work, children and an everyday fast paced life living apart.

The month of May ended and in the middle of June, Essa knew that she was pregnant. She discussed the pregnancy with Tony. They both agreed that she should should have the child. They also decided to get married as soon as possible.

Tony contacted the Chaplin on the Navy base and they set up a date to be married in a small ceremony in the little Chapel.

Francis was Tony's Best Man and Katy was the Matron of Honor. Only family and a few friends attended. They also all went to dinner in South San Francisco at a very nice Italian Restaurant called Bertolucci's.

Both Essa and Tony could not be more happy. They found a nice home in San Bruno on Santa Lucia Ave. It was close to El Crystal Elementary School, Parkside Junior High and Capuchino High School.

It also happened to be walking distance to the City Park. The park had a swimming pool, a War Memorial Recreation Center, plenty of tennis courts, several baseball fields for little league teams and many places to Bar-b- Que and have picnics. The children would spend much of their time in all of those places with the many neighborhood children having fun.

Mitchel John was born on the seventh of February. Tony wanted to name him after his Marine friend Rich, but that was Janessa's ex husbands name. So they named him Mitchel John. Most people would end up calling him MJ or Mitch but Tony would always call him Duke!

The five of them settled into a very comfortable life.

Tony would leave every morning to work at the Navy Base as a Jag lawyer. Essa loved being a stay at home mother. She would become a Cub Scout leader for Frank's Den. She organized many activities helping the seven scouts in her Den get their patches and prepare them to become Boy Scouts. She volunteered at El Crystal Elementary School and became active with the Parents Club. MJ went every where with her. She was trilled to have him in all of their lives. He was a happy and healthy little boy.

Tony bought season tickets to the San Francisco Forty Niner games for the 1966 season. He would continue to be a season ticket holder when they moved the games to Candlestick Park . Essa, Frank ,Katy and Tony each had a seat on the wooden benches in Kezar Stadium. They sat in Section OO row 63. All of the surrounding seats were always filled with the same people at every game. The "Fireman" sat next to Tony for every game. He brought his large transistor radio so that all could hear Lon Simmons call the game. The Niners under Head Coach Jack Christensen finished with a 6 and 6 record with two ties. John Brodie was the quarterback passing for 2,810 yards and 16 touchdowns. Unfortunately, he also threw 22 interceptions! Ken Willard who played fullback, rushed for 763 yards ,caught 42 passes and scored 7 over all touchdowns. John David Crow added over 800 total yards and four touchdowns. Brodie had two favorite targets to throw to from the wide receiver positions. Dave Parks caught 66 passes and Bernie Casey added 50. Future Hall of Fame players, Jimmy Johnson and Dave Wilcox lead the defense along with Charlie Kruger and Tony's favorite Roland Lakes. Janessa really liked John Brodie, Katy was a fan of Dave Parks and Frank would always stand with his legs crossed and hands on his hips just like Dave Wilcox did. They would also spend Sunday mornings watching the road games on KPIX channel 5. They would listen to Bob Fouts and Lon Simmons. After the TV games, Frank and Katy would head to the park for pick up football games with the boys in the neighborhood. Frank was a good running back and Katy was always Dave Parks.

Frank and Katy changed schools when they started at Parkside Junior High. They would walk to school through San Bruno Park. Even when it rained! There would be times when they would be late because the San Francisco Warriors practiced at the War Memorial Gym. They were big basketball fans, as was Janessa. Getting a chance to watch players like Wilt Chamberlain, Nate Thurmond, Tom Meschery and Rick Berry practice was too hard to pass up. They would get in trouble at school but Janessa understood!

Sports in this home were very important. Frank would eventually play football, basketball and baseball at Capuchino High School. Title Nine came into effect in 1972. Katy would be a cheerleader during the fall. In the winter she played Varsity basketball and she ran Track in the spring. All of these events kept both Janessa and Tony very busy. Just the way they liked it.

Tony and Duke would always walk to St. Roberts Catholic Church on Sunday mornings. They enjoyed the time together as they walked through the park. Duke was a very smart little boy. He was not a big kid. Small compared to others his age. But he had something that others didn't. A competitive sprite. He competed in the classroom as well as on any ball field.

Tony eventually retired from the Marine Corp as a Colonel. He had thought of calling Pete Pardini. If he could work for Frank Sinatra from his home, he might be interested. Unfortunately for Tony, he would have to move to Palm Springs to work with Frank and his lawyers. He had moved too much already in his life, he would stay where he was at and enjoy life in San Bruno.

The pain at nights that he suffered slowed but never went away. He would always avoid Forth of July celebrations. The Fireworks and firecrackers would bring back memories that he didn't want. New Year Eve celebrations were avoided also. Other than making an early day trip to Coit Tower, Tony and Janessa stayed away from the noise of late night parties. The children often asked him about his past. He had many stories but he never discussed his time in battle. He talked about time on Maui. How beautiful and peaceful it was without mention of Keke. The children became interested in Salem Oregon and they even took a summer vacation to Oregon. They liked it and even thought of attending college at Willamette University but once they visited Washington DC, They made up their minds that Georgetown was the place to be.

MJ aka Duke eventually followed Tony's footsteps and went straight into the Marine Corp. for his lifetime career, becoming a Master Sergeant.

After retirement, Janessa and Tony enjoyed morning walks in the park. On one beautiful cool fall morning walk, they sat down on a bench overlooking the creek that flowed through the park. Each dressed in blue jeans and wool sweaters that matched.

"Tony. We need to plan a trip to Tahoe. Catch a show at Harrahs and enjoy the beach for a week."

Tony smiled

"That would be nice. It sure has changed though. Nothing better than sitting on beach with you. Lets do it."

"We can play some blackjack and I can teach you how to play craps!"

"Tony?" Janessa looked into Tony's eyes

"Yes !"

"Isn't great that we gave each other a second chance!"

"Without a doubt" They then kissed each other and sat quietly on the bench holding hands.

www.ingramcontent.com/pod-product-compliance
Lightning Source LLC
Chambersburg PA
CBHW070620310726
48982CB00001B/138

* 9 7 8 1 9 6 6 4 7 7 6 0 0 *